Title: Catch that Dog!

Author: Will Taylor

On-Sale Date: April 5, 2022

Format: Jacketed Hardcover

ISBN: 978-1-338-74595-5

Price: $17.99 US

Ages: 8–12

Grades: 3–7

LOC Number: Available

Length: 240 pages

Trim: 5-1/2 x 8-1/4 inches

Classification: Juvenile Fiction:
Animals; Pets / Humorous Stories

---------------- *Additional Formats Available* --------------

Ebook ISBN: 978-1-338-74597-9

Scholastic Press
An Imprint of Scholastic Inc.
557 Broadway, New York, NY 10012
For information, contact us at:
tradepublicity@scholastic.com

Catch that DOG!

WILL TAYLOR

SCHOLASTIC PRESS / NEW YORK

All rights reserved. Published by Scholastic Press, an imprint of
Scholastic Inc., *Publishers since 1920*. SCHOLASTIC, SCHOLASTIC PRESS, and
associated logos are trademarks and/or registered trademarks of
Scholastic Inc.
The publisher does not have any control over and does not assume any
responsibility for author or third-party websites or their content.
No part of this publication may be reproduced, stored in a retrieval
system, or transmitted in any form or by any means, electronic,
mechanical, photocopying, recording, or otherwise, without written
permission of the publisher. For information regarding permission,
write to Scholastic Inc., Attention: Permissions Department,
557 Broadway, New York, NY 10012.
While inspired by real events and historical characters, this is a work
of fiction and does not claim to be historically accurate or portray
factual events or relationships. Please keep in mind that references to
actual persons, living or dead, business establishments, events, or
locales may not be factually accurate, but rather fictionalized
by the author.
Library of Congress Cataloging-in-Publication Data available
ISBN 978-1-338-74595-5

10 9 8 7 6 5 4 3 2 1   22 23 24 25 26

Printed in the U.S.A.   66
First edition, April 2022
Book design by Maeve Norton

DEDICATION TK

One
A GIRL LIKE YOU

Like most kids, Joanie Dayton had a favorite number. Hers was five, so here are five useful things to know about Joanie:

1. She was ten years old.
2. She was an only child (and often lonely).
3. Both her eyes were brown, but her right eye showed everything crisp and clear while her left eye stayed permanently out of focus. She didn't mind, though, since that was how she'd always seen the world. She called them her *sharp* eye and her *soft* eye, and sometimes switched between them just for fun.
4. She had a secret talent she'd kept hidden from everyone ever.
5. She was about to get in trouble. Again.

"Joanne Louise Dayton, what is that racket?!"

The clatter of cans echoing from the alley off Main Street ended abruptly, and a pale girl with messy brown hair appeared, a broom clutched in her hands. It was warm for early May in Banbridge, New Jersey, and the girl wore patched overalls over a T-shirt that was at least two sizes too big. The overalls and shirt were covered in soot, oil, dirt, and paint. So were the girl's skinny arms.

Her mother, leaning out the door of Dayton Family Shoeshine, scowled at the sight of her.

"Joanie," she said, in that tone the girl knew all too well.

Joanie risked a glance up. She'd always thought her mother was pretty enough to be a film star, but life had made other plans. Sylvia Dayton—*wasn't that a perfect name for a movie star?*—had ended up with a husband who shined shoes, an aching back, and a daughter she'd never entirely wanted. All of it showed now on her tired, frowning face.

Joanie's heart sank. It had been exactly one hundred and thirteen days since her mother had smiled at her. She'd counted them.

"How did you get so filthy, girl?" Mrs. Dayton demanded. "What on earth were you doing?"

Joanie raised the broom, full of explanations. "There was a cat, Ma! It got stuck under those old broken crates!"

"A cat?" Her mother shuddered. "Any cat scrounging in

2

that alley is a disgusting stray, and you're not to go near it. You understand me?"

"Yes, ma'am." Joanie bit her lip to stop herself from talking, but was as unsuccessful as always. She burst out two seconds later with, "But it was sniffling and crying! I only climbed in and poked with my broom to try and let it out. I didn't know there was paint in those cans and—"

"Joanie—"

"I thought that it needed a friend!"

Mrs. Dayton sighed and pressed three fingers to her forehead.

The evening sunlight falling over town didn't reach their dingy corner of Main Street, but Joanie still thought her mother almost glowed. She closed her sharp eye for a moment, and sure enough, her soft eye revealed the truth: Underneath all that sadness, Sylvia Dayton gleamed around the edges.

"Let me guess," Mrs. Dayton said. "You thought you could rescue this cat and it would become your best friend and love you forever. Is that about right?" She didn't pause for an answer. "You don't understand anything about the world, Joanie. You still think you'll wake up one day and be a princess. Well, it's time you grew out of that. Good things aren't going to fall out of the sky for a girl like you. You've got nothing coming unless you learn to quit dreaming, work hard, and behave as you should."

"Yes, ma'am." Joanie let out a long, silent breath and looked past the open door into the familiar space of the shop, her family's second home. Two big shoeshine chairs sat against one wall, their worn leather arms carefully polished to make the rich people feel comfortable. Across from them was the workbench for eyelet replacement, sole patching, and good-as-new stitching. Right at the back of the shop, her father, Paul Dayton, folded like a newspaper and almost as gray, sat at the tiny counter totaling up the day's meager earnings.

Joanie's heart twinged, and something dense and heavy seemed to settle onto her shoulders, pressing her feet down into the pavement.

"Now go home and get yourself clean," said Mrs. Dayton, satisfied that her daughter had gotten the message. "No more running after filthy animals." She seized the ragged broom and stepped into the shop, then turned back. "And take the side streets, won't you? What will people think of us if they see you looking like that?"

The door closed with a groan and a snap, and Joanie was left all alone on the darkening sidewalk. She examined her reflection in the window, eyeing herself with first one eye, then the other. She sniffed, tugging at her tangled hair and smoothing the sleeves of her shirt. She wasn't *that* dirty, she thought. And anyway, she *couldn't* take the side streets, no matter what her mother said. Not right before dinner-time. All the rich kids would be out, playing in front of their houses, and the Archers and the Payton-Prices never missed a chance to tease the poorest girl in town. The last time she'd passed the Archer boys' yard, they'd thrown rotten crab apples. They were all good shots.

The heavy weight was still pressing down, but Joanie Dayton put her shoulders back, lifted her chin, and started along Main Street for home.

Behind her, a grateful little animal peeked out from the jumbled darkness of the alley, sniffed at the cool evening air, and followed.

Two
A CURTSY

The little animal was a dog—a gray toy poodle, to be exact—and his name was Masterpiece. Here are five important things to know about Masterpiece:

1. He'd never quite liked the name Masterpiece, but that was what the man with the gold rings, Count Pulaski, had always called him. It was even embroidered on the silk pillow Masterpiece sat on in the front window of Poodles, Inc., in New York City.

2. He was *extremely* famous. He had been featured in *Vogue* magazine, received a medal from the government of Haiti, and even eaten at the Ritz Hotel in Paris with the president of France.

3. He had once led an entire parade of poodles

right down the middle of Fifth Avenue, causing a media sensation and making him feel like the king of the world.

4. His thick haircut was Count Pulaski's own design. No pom-poms for this poodle! Masterpiece's look left his head, chest, shoulders, and legs thick and curly, like a gentlemanly lion.

5. He was very, *very* hungry.

Being very, very hungry was a new experience for Masterpiece. Every day for all six years of his life, he'd enjoyed lovely meals served like clockwork by the count or a waiter or one of the count's flowery-smelling friends. Not today, though. It had been hours since breakfast, and he was certainly getting acquainted with hunger now.

He'd hoped to find something to eat behind those crates in the alley—they had smelled mostly like food. Only it had turned out to be something else. Something . . . not fancy. Then when he'd tried to leave, a can of thick, harsh-smelling goo had tipped over him, and he'd become trapped. Very, very trapped.

His usual afternoons of waiter-served meals and embroidered cushions had never seemed as nice as they did right then. He jumped and dug and prodded and pushed, but nothing did any good. Eventually, he lay down, sadly pondering his choices, wishing he hadn't stepped out of that red-coated lady's car back at the gas station.

He wasn't normally the sort to explore without permission, but the lady hadn't closed her door all the way when she got out to pay, and with nothing to do and that silver-gray cat up front ignoring him for the entire ride, he'd been feeling a trifle bored. So, when that divine smell had come drifting by—rich and salty and crackling—well, he'd decided to be just a little daring and go sniff it out.

It had been a mild disappointment to discover the smell was only an old fried chicken bucket, and a giant shock to turn around and discover the car he'd been riding in was gone. The lady had driven off without him! That one small act of unleashed curiosity had left him abandoned, unfed, and, finally, trapped.

He'd been stuck in the alley for hours—long, hungry, lonely hours—when at last the girl had appeared. Masterpiece's first impression was that her clothes did not fit her properly, and she smelled like dirt and sweat, especially after she got down on her belly and began making swipes at him with that broom. But she made kind, soothing sounds as she did, and underneath the dirt and sweat, Masterpiece noticed she smelled an awful lot like sunshine.

Luckily, the girl got the biggest crates shifted before she abruptly ran off, and with a fair amount of unpleasant wriggling, Masterpiece had worked himself the rest of the way free. He'd been delighted to escape, of course, but also worried. The night was coming on, and he was very, very alone.

So, when he spotted the sunshine girl walking past, her head held high and her shoes tapping on the sidewalk, the only sensible thing to do was follow.

Sunshine Girl walked at a good pace, throwing in little dance steps every now and then. Masterpiece found that charming. So original of her! She slowed a few times: once to stare through the windows of a shop selling rather gaudy furniture and once to gaze longingly at a row of mannequins in sparkly dresses. Masterpiece cocked his head at that. Those dresses were wildly out of date. No one in the big city would be caught dead wearing anything so out of fashion. Did Sunshine Girl really not know?

The girl turned her head as she lingered over the last and sparkliest dress, and Masterpiece ducked out of sight into the doorway of Earl's Modern Home. He wasn't completely sure that she could help him yet. She smelled like sunshine, certainly, but not flowers. In his experience it was the people who smelled like flowers who had the best food and the most comfortable beds. The lady in the red coat, for instance, had smelled wonderfully of flowers. That was why he'd left Poodles, Inc., with her and gotten into her car in the first place, even though they'd never been introduced.

He peered out again in time to see Sunshine Girl hold both arms out at her sides, put one foot behind the other, and bend a graceful knee. Masterpiece's heart leapt. She was curtsying to the sparkly dress! Curtsying and sighing! Just like the fashionable ladies on TV! Just like a royal princess!

That settled it. Missing flower smell or not, Masterpiece was convinced: This girl had to be trustworthy.

Full of confidence, he left the shadows and trotted up to make her acquaintance.

"Oh!" Sunshine Girl was rising from a second curtsy when she spotted him, and she had to flail her arms to keep her balance. "Oh! Kitty!"

Masterpiece stopped.

He blinked.

He looked around. He did not see a kitty.

That was good. He'd only really gotten to know one cat before—Georgette, a prizewinning Manx owned by the king of Sweden. Despite being the same size, they had *not* seen eye to eye, and their disagreement on proper manners had almost started an international incident.

Well, cats were proud, standoffish animals; everybody knew that. The lady with the red coat's silver-gray companion hadn't even bothered to acknowledge his existence when they were sharing the same car. Although compared to Georgette, that had actually been an improvement.

"Kitty!" the girl said again, looking directly at him, and Masterpiece, blinking, understood. "I'm so relieved you escaped! And hey, we're both covered in paint! Are you all right otherwise? Are you hurt? Are you cold? Are you hungry?"

Masterpiece was so happy to hear that last question, he forgot to be offended at being mistaken for a cat. He stood right up on his hind legs and nodded, his eyes shining.

The girl's face transformed, her smile as beautiful as her sunshiny smell. She had a gap between her front teeth.

"How are you doing that?" she gasped. "Clever kitty!"

Masterpiece lowered himself, settling into his most dignified sit. Enough was enough. He couldn't let this new friend go on thinking he was a cat. It wasn't proper.

"Woof," he said, as politely as he could. He used his indoor volume, his special guest accent, and the hollow-O sound that most flower-smelling humans liked best.

The message was successful. "Oh!" cried the girl. "You're not a kitty! You're a doggy!"

Masterpiece repeated his nod, then let out the smallest, faintest whine. His stomach was so empty it was becoming quite upsetting. Which was ironic, he realized as his insides groaned, since it was chasing a delicious food smell that had gotten him into this mess in the first place.

"You really are hungry, aren't you?" observed the girl, crinkling her eyebrows. "I am, too. I'm Joanie, by the way. Joanie Dayton. What's your name? Oh, I know you can't tell me. I just have so many questions! Do you have an owner? Where did you come from? How did you get stuck in that alley?" She gazed down at him, enraptured, then bit her lip.

"The thing is, my mom told me to stay away from you. But that *was* when we thought you were a cat. Ma can't get mad at me for helping a lost little doggy, can she? I mean, it wouldn't be right to leave you out here all hungry and covered in paint. Do you want to come home with me? Do you?"

Masterpiece, delighted, trotted in the tight circle that meant *Yes!*

The girl clapped her hands, her pretty brown eyes glowing. "Hooray! This will be fun! I've never had a friend over for supper before."

Side by side, the girl and the little dog set off, forgetting all about the window displays and shuttered shops of Main Street.

So neither of them saw the words appearing on the television screens shining out from Earl's Modern Home.

Prize Poodle Pinched!

"Masterpiece" Nabbed!

Dognappers on the Loose!

13

Neither of them saw the photograph of the small gray dog standing on his hind legs for a glossy fashion magazine shoot.

Neither of them saw the middle-aged man crying for the camera, wiping away his tears with a hand covered in gold rings.

Neither of them heard the breaking news:

World's Most Valuable Dog Goes Missing! Police Hunt Underway!

Three
A DISASTER

Ninety miles south of Banbridge, a light rain had begun to fall, making the streetlights shimmer on a powder-blue sedan rumbling steadily down Route 10.

A woman sat behind the wheel, humming along with the doo-wop music coming from the radio. She wore a tight blue dress with flared shoulders, fresh red lipstick, and black high heels. Brown curls wrapped her head and a dazzling diamond bracelet sparkled on her pale wrist. A red coat, a fashionably giant purse, and an equally fashionable silver-gray cat rested on the passenger seat beside her. The cat's name was Katerina. The woman's name was Holly Knickerbocker, and she was very famous.

Five glamorous things to know about Holly Knickerbocker:

1. Her column, appearing in only the best

newspapers, detailed every twist and turn of wealthy Manhattan society. She knew who was who, what was what, and the ins and outs of every intrigue, party, deal, and scandal.

2. The particular shade of powder-blue paint covering her car was provided courtesy of the one and only Tiffany's.

3. Her jasmine-heavy perfume, *Tres Chic L'Amour*, was custom blended exclusively for her in the oldest perfumery in Paris.

4. Her Manhattan apartment had its own private elevator.

5. The youngest of seven siblings, she had worked her way to the top through sheer personality, unbreakable will, and a famously ferocious way with words.

The road sang under Holly's tires as she glanced back over her shoulder. The little gray shape was still huddled behind the passenger seat.

"Come on now, Masterpiece," she said. She had a bright, powerful voice, like a trumpet. "You can stop hiding. Everything is wonderful. I'm taking you on a quick vacation, that's all."

Katerina yawned. The topic of Masterpiece bored her

considerably. Why anyone would get excited over a common gray poodle—a common gray *toy* poodle at that—was beyond her, especially when there were cats like her in the world. Katerina was a Russian blue and had the aristocratic pedigree to prove it. She had been born regal. No dog, no matter how thoroughly shampooed and pampered and trained, could ever aspire to her level of importance. It was embarrassing to see her human so giddy over the thing. Katerina yawned again, very pointedly, and tugged the expensive, perfume-scented red coat into a more comfortable shape.

Holly hummed happily, bopping her head to the music. Everything really *was* wonderful. 1953 was going to be her year. Who cared if younger society columnists were popping up everywhere? Who cared if people said she was losing her touch?

She would show them.

Not one of those fools suspected she could pull off a heist like this.

She herself couldn't quite believe how well it had gone. The most valuable dog in the world! All she'd had to do was saunter in wearing an old gray wig and granny glasses, wait until no one was looking, order the little mutt to come with her, and walk out. She hadn't even had to face down that fake celebrity Count Pulaski.

Masterpiece had trotted out of Poodles, Inc., as politely as you could please, hopped into Holly's waiting car, and curled up like a prince.

"Bet you thought I was a chauffeur, didn't you?" she called to the back seat. "You're used to that high life, huh, kid?"

There was no reply. Katerina flicked her tail and smiled. She thought of Holly as her chauffeur, too.

"Well, don't worry," Holly went on. "You'll be back soon enough. We'll just unwind at my beach house for a few days, then when the search for you is going good and hot, we'll whisk home and I'll 'find' you! Can you imagine? What a turn of events! *Missing Masterpiece rescued by society queen Holly Knickerbocker*—the papers will have a field day! We're gonna be the world's biggest stars!"

She drummed her fingers happily on the wheel, visions of her triumph flashing through her mind like the streetlights flashing over the car.

"Say, whatever happened to you back at that gas station?" she asked after another few miles. "You were perched up all pretty and polite before. Then we hit—what was that little nowhere town called? Burbage? Binridge? Something there must've scared you silly. If I couldn't see your fuzzy little behind tucked down there by my travel bag, I might think you'd run off! Ha ha!"

Holly drove on, the music somehow not quite filling the silence in the car anymore. A minute or two later she noticed she was chewing her lower lip.

Frowning slightly, she took a hand off the wheel and reached back, one eye on the road while her fingers groped for the soft curls of the little poodle's hair.

Katerina's ears twitched in amusement coupled with resigned irritation. She knew what was coming, and that it wouldn't be pretty.

The sudden screech of braking tires seared through the night. Cars in the oncoming lane veered out of the way, their drivers shouting as Holly Knickerbocker's powder-blue sedan swerved and spun, finally skidding to a shuddering halt on the verge.

Holly was out of her seat before the car stopped moving, blood pounding in her ears as she dove into the back, searching frantically.

But there was no poodle anywhere.

The dog was gone.

Her manicured nails clenched around the wig she'd found under the passenger seat—the very wig she'd worn to steal Masterpiece from his owner. It must have fallen from her travel bag somewhere along the way.

She'd been talking to a wig. A half-dollar costume wig. For hours.

Anger boiled over inside Holly. The little mutt had to have jumped out when she was filling up. What *was* that town? Burpridge? Borridge? One thing was certain: She wouldn't be sleeping in her comfortable beach house tonight. She had to get back to that gas station. Right now.

Katerina sighed as Holly pulled a puddle-spraying U-turn, sending her gleaming sedan speeding back along the highway.

More fuss. Always more fuss. She herself had been perfectly happy to see the dog go, but now Holly was going to make a thing of it, and Katerina, as always, would be the one to suffer the inconvenience.

She dug her claws into the giant purse and pulled a fold of the red coat over her head. Humans did make good chauffeurs and attendants, but in the end, even the best of them were drearily predictable.

Four
A BATH

Joanie pointed a paint-stained finger as she and her new friend rounded the final corner. "Look," she said. "We're almost home!"

Their walk had taken them all the way down Main Street, right on Park, left on Twelfth, and finally across the rusted train tracks onto Nickerson Street.

The Daytons, Masterpiece learned, lived at the far end of the street, where there were no other houses and no bulbs in the streetlamps. Their house was one story, a little lop-sided, and painted with a dusty patchwork of tan and green and gray. Masterpiece thought it looked cornered, crouching there awkwardly between a warehouse on one side and a gravel lot full of disused oil cans on the other. After living in the city all his life, he had no idea houses could be so small or look so vulnerable.

Still, it was where Joanie lived, and he liked the house for that. He was already feeling fond of his new acquaintance, with her sunshine smell, her dancing walk, and the way she'd sighed looking at those dresses.

"Ma and Pa will be home soon," Joanie said as they walked up the cracked concrete path. "I'm in trouble already for getting dirty, so we'd better get straight in the tub. I know you're hungry, but we have to wait for them for dinner anyway, and Ma'll be more friendly if you're bright and shiny when she meets you."

They reached the dark front door and Joanie unlocked it, waved Masterpiece inside, and flicked on the lights.

Masterpiece looked around curiously. The Dayton home was shabby and worn, but clearly cared for. The peeling linoleum floor was spotless. The mismatched furniture was neatly arranged. Even the faded pink-and-cream wallpaper showed signs of careful patching, though it was hard to tell in the light of the few dim bulbs. The one thing the small house seemed to have plenty of was shadows.

Masterpiece sniffed. The smell was fascinating: potatoes and onions, scrubbed wood, old glue and wet wool, all softened by an undercurrent of harsh lavender soap.

"Okay, I'll show you to the bathroom," said Joanie, slipping off her shoes, "and then I'll be right back."

Masterpiece found himself ushered into a cramped little

room containing a sink, a toilet, and a bathtub, all done in an unpleasant banana yellow. Joanie pulled a shoelace hanging from the wall, and a solitary bulb buzzed into life on the ceiling. The room was as clean as could be, but that couldn't hide the cracks in the wall or the rust gathered around the pipes.

Masterpiece had never spent time in Count Pulaski's bathroom, but he'd caught glimpses, and it had been a grand suite of marble and gold taps and the constant aroma of eau de cologne. Certainly nothing like this.

Masterpiece imagined Count Pulaski would have felt disgust at the size and state of the Daytons' bathroom. The count had strong opinions regarding the proper way to live. But all Masterpiece felt was . . . curiosity. This was a new part of the world he was seeing; a whole new way of life. And it occurred to him that if it was good enough for Sunshine Girl, maybe it didn't matter what anyone else thought.

Joanie returned a minute later wearing a patched cotton dress that only barely reached her knees. Her overalls and T-shirt were bundled in her arms. Masterpiece tilted his head and studied the dress.

"What, this?" Joanie said, noticing. "It got too small for me last year, but Ma says it's good enough to wear for housework. And these"—she dumped her armful of fabric into the empty bathtub—"are definitely going to take some work."

Masterpiece propped his paws on the side of the tub

as Joanie turned on the faucet. Water thundered in.

"I hope you don't mind being in the same water as my clothes," Joanie said over the roar. "The way I see it, we're all the same sort of dirty, so it won't matter. I'll get you clean first, then do my things. But hey, what about what *you're* wearing, doggy?"

Masterpiece had only a second to wonder what she meant before Joanie's hands were digging into the thick, curly hair around his neck.

"Oh!" she said in surprise. "Where's your collar? Why don't you have one?"

Too distracted to answer, Masterpiece pressed into her fingers, and Joanie obligingly scratched.

"I thought for sure someone owned you," she said. "But maybe you're a real stray? That would be okay because then I might get to keep you!"

Masterpiece leaned against her, his eyes closed in bliss. He loved having his neck scratched, and it had been a long, *long* time. Count Pulaski thought scritches were "common," and hardly anyone else dared to give him more than a pat on the head in case the count got mad. Joanie's gentle fingers felt like heaven, and the first good reason he'd found to have gotten out of that car.

As for collars, the truth was he had plenty—some decorated with real diamonds, some made just for him by the world's greatest fashion designers—but he'd never worn one in his window seat at Poodles, Inc. What would be the point when he was safe inside? His job was to sit there and look handsome. When the lady in the red coat had led him out to her car without one, he'd just assumed they were heading somewhere he wouldn't need it.

Joanie gave Masterpiece one last really good scratch under his chin and turned back to the tub, which was nearly halfway full. She shut off the water.

"Okay, doggy. Let's get you clean!"

Masterpiece was used to following directions, so he hopped in all by himself, making Joanie laugh when she got splashed. He turned in a careful circle, getting his bearings in the ugly yellow tub. The water was lukewarm—certainly not the perfect temperature he was used to—but he didn't mind too much. At least a bath would distract him from his gurgling stomach.

Joanie gently scooped water over him, then worked up a lather with a bar of hard, flaking soap and began scrubbing away.

Masterpiece quickly realized this was not going to be a professional puppy pampering. Not by a long shot. The dried paint snagged in his fur, the soap stung his eyes, and Joanie's washing technique was rather rough around the abdomen.

But Joanie also hummed while she worked, and never

once stopped smiling. As the bath went on, Masterpiece felt a warm glow for the girl building in his heart. Joanie seemed so happy to have company, and to have someone to take care of. After a lifetime among famous, fancy people, it was surprisingly nice to be around someone who focused on the simple things that made up the bits and pieces of a day. Someone who danced when she walked, and hummed when she washed, and clapped her two rough hands when she was happy. He had never met anyone quite like her, and he was beginning to think she was rather marvelous.

"You're so patient, doggy," Joanie said as Masterpiece held up his paws for her to wash. "I'm not the best at being patient. Maybe I can learn from you!" She beamed at him in the chilly light. "I mean, if you want to stay, that is. Would you maybe want that? Since nobody owns you? I'd have to get Ma and Pa to say yes, but if they did, we could be best friends! Wouldn't that be the best thing ever? What do you think?"

Masterpiece blinked up at her from under his crown of soap bubbles.

Stay? Here in this curious house? With Joanie?

Just considering it made his stomach go all swirly, but one thing was suddenly certain: After six identical years, his life as he'd known it was about to change. One way or another. For better or for worse.

And that was terribly exciting.

Five
A HAIRCUT

When her new friend was as clean and washed and scrubbed as Joanie could manage, she rinsed him off in fresh water from the tap and pulled him out of the tub.

The sweet little dog gave her a smile, then shook enthusiastically from nose to tail, making Joanie laugh as water flew across the bathroom. She pulled a thin towel from under the sink and rubbed him down, laughing all over again at the sight of his fur poofing up like a dandelion.

Joanie examined him first with her sharp right eye, then with her soft left. "Well, you definitely smell better, doggy," she said. "But you're still all marked up. That paint really soaked in deep." She sighed. "I guess I'll have to give you a haircut when I've got the washing done."

She went back to the tub of graying water and scrubbed

out her clothes, washing the paint from her own arms and face as she did. She let the water drain, squeezed everything out, then dried herself with the damp towel.

She was rummaging under the sink for scissors when noises sounded from the kitchen.

"Hi, Ma! Hi, Pa!" she called. "I'm in here!"

A moment later there was a tap on the door.

"Joanie? Are you getting cleaned up?"

Joanie made a *shh* gesture at the little dog, a grin pulling at her cheeks. "Yes, Ma!"

"Good. Be sure you tidy the bathroom when you're finished. I don't want to see any water on the floor."

"Yes, Ma!"

"Supper in twenty minutes; no dawdling."

"Yes, Ma!"

Joanie finally located a pair of heavy, thick-handled scissors and returned to her friend.

"Okay," she said, settling on her knees. "I hope you don't mind getting a haircut, doggy—you're going to need one to look clean, or there's no way my ma will let you stay."

The dog tilted his fuzzball head, then gave the tiniest, politest little bark in the world and stood up straight.

"That sounds like yes to me," Joanie said, beaming. She patted the tub, and just like that, the dog hopped back in. He immediately turned another circle, and Joanie felt her heart squeeze. For a dog nobody seemed to want, he was awfully sweet.

"Here we go!" she said, brandishing the scissors, and the haircut began.

As Joanie snipped and clipped and the corners of the tub slowly filled with gray curls, she found herself telling the dog about her life. She started by telling him about her own haircuts, done by her mom out in the yard, and how the family used the tub for all their washing since the laundromat in town was too expensive. That led to her talking about being poor, and how the other kids in town acted like it was something you could catch like the flu, which was why she didn't really have any friends.

She tried to do as little cutting as possible at first, but the paint had really gotten in there, and it quickly became clear she was going to have to give the little guy an all-over trim.

But even when Joanie took her scissors as close as they could go, stains and splotches still covered her new friend's coat. Combined with his super-short hair, he looked almost like a miniature dalmatian.

The dog was wonderfully patient while Joanie trimmed, but he did look consideringly at the pile of fur collecting at his feet once or twice. He even leaned down his cute button nose to sniff it.

"It's a lot, I know, I'm sorry," Joanie said. "But at least it'll grow back clean!"

The smell of onion soup wafted through from the kitchen just as she was finishing up, and she felt her stomach rumble. The little dog must have heard, because he looked directly into her face and gave the gentlest whine, his eyes wide and shining.

"I know, me too," Joanie said. "I'm almost done, buddy. Then hopefully everything will go well with my parents, and we can get some dinner!"

At last, the haircut was complete, and Joanie gave the dog a vigorous brush with her fingers, then cleaned up the mess they'd made in the tub. All the hair went into a metal can in the corner, the towel wiped up the water on the floor and walls, and everything was done.

"Ready?" Joanie asked. Her hands felt all jittery, and there were butterflies dancing in her stomach alongside the hunger. The dog, catching her mood, flicked his ears and shifted from paw to paw.

She really hoped she could talk her parents into this.

Joanie took a deep breath. She opened the door.

"Ma! Pa!" she called, striding out of the bathroom, the little dog at her heels. "Look who followed me home!"

Six
AN ARGUMENT

The grown-up voices stopped as Joanie and her companion entered the kitchen. Her mother, wearing an apron over her work dress, turned from the stove.

"What are you shouting abou—" she began, then cut off, her pretty, tired face flaring open in shock. "Oh, no. Absolutely not! I am not having dogs in this house. Do you hear me?" She pointed a wooden spoon at the freshly washed pair. "Where did you even find—" Mrs. Dayton's expression somehow became even angrier. "Joanne Louise Dayton, if this is the animal you saw in that filthy alley . . ."

She advanced, brandishing the spoon. Joanie swooped down and picked up the dog, shielding him in her skinny arms.

"But he's clean now, Ma! Promise! I gave him a really good bath!"

"You washed that thing in our *bathtub*?!"

"He's my friend! And he really is clean! Just smell him."

Joanie held out the dog, but her mother did not take her up on the offer.

"What could possibly have made you think this animal was yours to keep? He could already have a home for all you know. You might have stolen someone's pet!"

Joanie had been worried about this part. "I know he doesn't have a home," she admitted, "because he doesn't have a collar."

Her mother's reaction was just what Joanie had feared.

"That means he's a stray! That's even worse! I want him out of this house, girl! Now!"

"But he's my friend!" Joanie repeated, clutching the dog close again. She didn't like arguing with her mother, but she was not about to give up. Not just like that. "And he's really well behaved even if no one owns him. I can't turn him out—he could starve! Or get hit by a car! Or get eaten by a bigger dog! I promise I'll pay for his food and medicine and everything out of my allowance. He needs someone who cares to look after him." She didn't understand why that last point felt so important, but it did.

"You think you can look after a dog?" Joanie's mother leaned down so they were almost nose to nose, the little animal blinking between them. "Or that we can afford one on top of everything else? The answer is no. Absolutely, no more arguing, for the last time—"

"Sylvia."

All three of their heads turned. Mr. Dayton, completely forgotten, was standing in the corner with his hands in his pockets. He looked as rumpled as his shirt, as over-stretched as his thin gray suspenders. The wrinkles crowding his tired eyes mirrored the sparse hair scattered across his head.

"Sylvia," he said again, this time giving Joanie's mother the faintest smile. "Let her keep it."

Joanie gasped and squeezed the little dog to her chest.

Mrs. Dayton's spoon almost flew out of her hand. "Paul, no. This family does not have the time or money for a pet."

Joanie's father crossed the room and put his arms around his wife. He held her very gently, whispering into the hair pinned up against her ears. Joanie could not make out what he was saying, but as he spoke, all the fight seemed to drain out of her mother.

Mr. Dayton stepped back, and Mrs. Dayton turned to look down at her only child and the dog in her arms.

There was a long pause, and then, "Oh, all right." Sylvia Dayton did not smile, but she reached out and grasped her husband's hand.

Joanie gave a cheer. The little dog gave a happy squeak as she kissed him.

"But there are rules!" Joanie's mother's expression had gone back to stern. "First, no barking allowed. *None.* You both hear me?" She waved the spoon.

Joanie nodded, promising her new dog would be good and polite and quiet.

"And he sleeps in your room, nowhere else!"

"Yes, yes, thank you!" said Joanie.

"And you're responsible for walking him in the morning and evening and picking up his mess!"

"Yes, yes!"

"And you'll be putting your allowance toward his food and any medicine he might need. *All* your allowance. From now on."

Joanie nodded. It would be a sacrifice giving up the little she had, but she already loved the sweet dog that much.

"Don't think your father or I will pick up any slack!" her mother warned. "Goodness knows we have enough to do already. The first time—the very first time—that animal becomes a problem, he's gone. Do you hear me, Joanie Dayton?"

"Yes, ma'am!" Joanie would have promised the world in that moment to be allowed to keep her friend.

"Hmph." Mrs. Dayton folded her arms, the spoon rising

like a sword against her shoulder. She regarded the pair of them. "Well, I suppose he'd better have some supper along with the rest of us. I'll see what I can find."

Poking out from under Joanie's elbow, the little dog's tail became a blur.

Seven
A SECRET

The humans ate first.

Masterpiece, sent to wait in the corner, supposed he could understand why; he was a last-minute dinner guest, after all. But understanding didn't do much to help his patience as the three Daytons gathered around their small table to slurp onion soup and chew canned green beans and crunch through five pale, crumbly crackers each.

"All right, then," Mrs. Dayton said at last, getting wearily to her feet as Joanie cleared the table. "Food for the dog."

Masterpiece waited, his mouth watering, as Mrs. Dayton bustled around the kitchen. When she returned, she set a chipped ceramic bowl at his feet.

He sniffed the contents. Hmm. Mushy oats, a few old peas, two of those crumbly crackers, chicken skin with feathery bits, and some sort of steamed root. Beets, maybe? And all mashed up together. How very odd. Normally he was served one bowl for moist food, one bowl for dry, and one for delicacies—those came in the fine china dish with blue fleurs-de-lis painted around the rim. He had certainly never dined like this, all out of one broken bowl, down on the floor.

Then again, he was terribly hungry.

"Look, Ma! He likes it!" Joanie cheered.

Masterpiece, chewing, didn't think he would have gone quite *that* far. He had never had cold oatmeal before. He had never had feathery chicken skin. He had never had steamed beets. And he did not think he'd like to try any of them ever again.

He'd tasted peas before, once, as a sort of lovely, peppery mash on delicate potato blinis topped with caviar. That had been at the Ritz in Paris, the day he first met the film star Rita Hayworth, who had smelled like an entire rose garden blooming under moonlight. These peas did not quite live up to that memory.

Still, he was a guest; and there was etiquette to consider.

Masterpiece ate his meal as politely as he could. And as quickly. Though as his empty belly quieted, he did notice that this plain food worked just the same as fancy food, in the end. Particularly when you had started out very, very hungry.

"Wash the bowl out when he's done," Mrs. Dayton said to Joanie. "Then fill it with water. You can keep it in your room tonight. Starting tomorrow we'll buy some real dog food, and *you'll* be in charge of feeding him, remember." She stared down at Masterpiece. "What is he, anyway? Some kind of terrier?"

"I don't know," Joanie said. "Maybe! He had poofy hair before, but I had to take it all off during his haircut."

"I'm surprised he let you do that. You're lucky not to be at the hospital getting stitches for a dog bite."

Masterpiece glanced up, shocked. He had never bitten anyone in his life! And he was actually exceedingly accustomed to haircuts, since Count Pulaski insisted his signature look be trimmed and maintained every three days, keeping his gray hair thick and curly around his chest and head and rear.

He hadn't minded this most recent haircut much at all. Joanie didn't have his usual stylist's flair with the scissors, true, but then his usual stylist had never scratched his neck.

Anyway, as Joanie had noted, it would all grow back.

When every scrap of food was gone, Masterpiece looked up at Mrs. Dayton and wagged his tail to say thank you. Wagging felt strange after his haircut. In fact, he felt rather chilly all over. He wondered what he looked like. He was certain he looked *nothing* like a terrier, at least. Imagine!

He examined the dining room while Joanie ran off to clean his bowl, much more able to indulge his curiosity now his belly was full.

Mr. Dayton had pulled out a crumpled magazine and was reading on one side of the table. Mrs. Dayton was settled across from him, sewing a patch on a pair of pants, sharing the light of the overhead lamp. Apparently, this was what the Daytons did after dinner. There was no music playing, no tinkle of cocktail glasses or shining dessert trays, no dancing.

Masterpiece cocked his head, trying to imagine days and weeks and years of this. It was certainly peaceful. But then why did the two grown-ups still smell so weary, and forlorn, and resigned?

"Come on, doggy," Joanie called, returning from the kitchen. She hefted his water bowl in one hand and patted her leg with the other. "I want to show you my room!"

The two of them had already turned away when Mr. Dayton's quiet voice tiptoed across the room. "What's his name, dear?"

Joanie stopped in her tracks.

She looked down at Masterpiece, who peered back up at her curiously.

He was going to get a new name? How fascinating!

Joanie's forehead wrinkled as she looked at him. He could almost hear her brain whirring.

Then her eyes lit up, and her face broke into a huge smile.

"Lucky!" she said. "His name is Lucky, because I'm lucky to have him."

Masterpiece thought his heart might leap out of his chest at the lovely compliment, and he did a little hopping dance so Joanie would know. He still felt like Masterpiece inside, but if his Sunshine Girl wanted to call him Lucky, he didn't mind a bit.

Joanie's father nodded from across the table as the two friends headed on their way.

"Don't spill that water, Joanie!" Mrs. Dayton called, her eyes flicking up from her sewing. "You'll slip and fall and break your leg. And there'll be no keeping that dog around then."

Joanie gripped the bowl with both hands, and Masterpiece followed her out of the kitchen. They returned to the tiny hall, passed the bathroom and what smelled like the parents' bedroom, and arrived at a small, dark space at the very back of the house.

"Ta-da!" Joanie said, pressing a light switch with her elbow. "Welcome to my room!"

Masterpiece blinked in surprise. He had seen closets bigger than Joanie's bedroom. It was more than half filled with her narrow twin bed, and judging by the size of the lone, beige curtain, the only window looked to be the size of a bread box.

The room was tidy and clean, at least. And cheerful in its way, just like Joanie. A patchwork quilt lay over the bed. Five rag dolls sat on an apple crate, which was filled with worn books and magazines. In the closet, which had no door, a modest collection of clothes hung in something close to rainbow order.

It was the walls, however, that commanded Masterpiece's full attention. Joanie had papered every inch of them with an enormous collage of people—film stars, TV stars, fashion models, jet-setters, and royals—all enjoying their fancy cars, fancy clothes, fancy meals, and fancy homes. Glossy or matte, black and white or color, Joanie had cut them out and pinned them up, a thousand glamorous moments floating like clouds all around her bed.

For Masterpiece, it was like looking at a montage from his own life. He actually had traveled the world in private airplanes, and sunbathed on yachts, and led parades, and dined at the very finest restaurants. And yes, it had all been very pleasant. How funny that his old routine had so completely captured Joanie's imagination. Was she hoping to do all these things herself someday? Did she think they would somehow make her happier?

Using enormous care, Joanie set the water bowl down in a corner. Masterpiece wasn't thirsty, but he sniffed politely anyway and took a few laps. For some reason this made Joanie squeal and flop down beside him to hug him around the middle. She certainly did get excited about the smallest things.

"I'm so happy we get to stay together, Lucky!" Joanie said into his remaining fur. "I never in a million years thought I would get a doggy of my own! We're going to have the happiest, best time!" She released him and sat up. "Okay, now I have to give you a tour, so you know about your new home. And so you can see all my treasures!"

It turned out Joanie liked giving tours. She showed Masterpiece her favorite patches in the patchwork quilt, and her favorite film stars on the walls. She told him the names of each of the rag dolls, and the name of her piggy bank with its one saved-up nickel. She showed him the books she'd gotten for free because they were unwanted after a library sale, and she showed him the dried autumn leaves she'd pasted with a special glue to the inside of her lampshade.

The contents of the closet turned out to be nothing much to comment on, just another pair of patched and worn overalls, a handful of T-shirts and coats, and four or five everyday school dresses. Joanie showed them all to

Masterpiece anyway, one by one. Then she reached right to the back of the closet and pulled out something wrapped in tissue.

Joanie beamed as Masterpiece cocked his head.

"This," she said, sweeping off the tissue, "is the grand finale. This is my most important, only-for-the-specialest-special-occasions *evening gown*."

Masterpiece eyed the garment. To his eyes, it was simply another dress. True, it was longer than the others, it had a black velvet bow at the back, and the pale blue fabric was puffy at the sleeves. And unlike her other dresses, it looked almost close to new. But none of that added up to an *evening gown*. Not as far as he could see. Evening gowns were grand affairs of silk and satin, meant for balls and operas and state dinners. He'd seen finer dresses on secretaries heading to the post office.

Joanie held the dress against herself, then raised her head and began a swirling walk back and forth across the room.

"Ma's only let me wear this out twice before," she said, doing a full twirl and curtsy. "But she also says I'm on the way to outgrowing it, so there better be more special occasions around here real soon!"

Joanie returned the dress to its tissue and the closet,

then declared she had shown off all her treasures and the tour was now over.

Masterpiece had enjoyed the tour. It seemed like something people should do more often. It was a wonderful way to turn an acquaintance into a real friend.

As for this room in this house possibly becoming his new home, well, he wasn't thinking that far ahead just yet. He was still coming to terms with how much his life had changed since he exited the red-coated lady's car. Stepping out alone like that might have been a huge mistake—it *had* gotten him abandoned in a parking lot—but then again, it might not. Things were certainly never dull here in the everyday world, where fancy and unfancy mixed together in such unexpected, interesting ways. Plus, he'd met his new friend Joanie, and she was nothing short of wonderful.

Perhaps that decision to be a little daring would turn out to have been the right move after all? His whole life he'd simply done exactly as he was told and things had worked out fine . . . but maybe things could be even better if he learned to rely on his instincts? To follow his own heart and nose?

Well, he would just have to stick around and see.

Right now, however, there was still one place in the room Joanie had not shown off on her tour, and Masterpiece's nose was telling him very curious things about it. Under the narrow twin bed, way back in the shadows, something smelled like Mr. Dayton, and the alley Masterpiece had gotten trapped in, and the floor of the New York Stock Exchange.

What it smelled like, very strongly, was shoe polish.

Too intrigued to resist, Masterpiece trotted over and poked his head under the bed, sniffing.

"Oh!" exclaimed Joanie. "Oh, Lucky. How did you know?"

She scrambled up to close her bedroom door, then flopped forward onto her belly beside Masterpiece. "This is my most secret thing in the world," she said in a stage whisper. "My biggest, most important secret ever."

Masterpiece blinked to show how interested he was.

"Not even my parents know, and you have to promise not to tell them, okay? You have to promise not to tell anybody ever."

Joanie leaned forward so her eyes were inches from Masterpiece's. He licked her nose to say yes, making her laugh.

"Okay, here goes!" She lay all the way flat, her cheek to the floor, and disappeared under the bed. When she emerged, a pile of cardboard and a low, thin box came with her.

Masterpiece had to work very hard not to bark in excitement as Joanie spread out the pile.

Paintings! The pile of cardboard was paintings! And the box was full of shoe polish tins, stained rags, and a collection of balding paintbrushes.

Most wonderful of all, the paintings—all in black, brown, tan, and gray—were good! They were very, very good! Masterpiece had been to enough museums to know a proper painting when he saw one, and these were extraordinary. They were *impressionist*, if he remembered the term right, a style that looked smudged or blurry up close but showed the soul of the subject brilliantly.

Most of the paintings were of women wearing gowns, just like in the pictures on Joanie's walls. The rest showed fancy cars and shining boats, sweeping bridges and sky-high buildings, all in Joanie's somber, earthy palette. Masterpiece couldn't say why, but he thought the paintings breathed, somehow. He could *feel* them.

"What do you think?" Joanie asked, propping especially fine paintings against her bed. "I don't know if they're any good, but I like making them." She twisted her hands together. "I've never shown anyone before. Ever."

Masterpiece didn't know when he'd felt more honored. He wished he could tell her just how brilliant they were. Though he did want to suggest that she paint a handsome dog now and then to fill out her portfolio. Dogs made everything better.

As if reading his thoughts, Joanie suddenly brightened.

"Oh! Hey, I know!" She seized a paintbrush from the box and held it high. "We need to mark this very important special occasion, Lucky, and I've got everything here. How about I paint a picture of *you*?"

Eight
A PORTRAIT

Joanie began piling up the paintings, reclaiming the little bit of floor space she had. Masterpiece watched them go by, admiring Joanie's skill, until one painting appeared that was so unexpected he had to put a paw out to stop it.

"What, Lucky?" Joanie halted her cleanup, looking down at the painting Masterpiece had selected. Her face changed. "Oh," she said softly. "That one."

The painting was in the same impressionist style as the others and showed a woman in a dove-gray evening gown, her hair an elegant swoop over one shoulder, her eyes gazing into the distance. She looked sad, beautiful, and utterly glamorous. She looked like the movie stars parading Joanie's walls. And she looked exactly like Sylvia Dayton.

"I think this is my favorite," Joanie said, picking it up and tracing a gentle finger along its edge. "Sometimes when my ma forgets to be worried, she looks like this. At least, *I* think she does. She's really, really pretty. And can I tell you another secret? Sometimes I hold it up and talk to it. Just tell it about my day at school, you know? It's almost like I'm telling her, and she's really listening."

Masterpiece looked from Joanie to the painting, then in the direction of the hall, hoping his question was clear.

"Oh, no," Joanie said, understanding. "I've never shown it to her. This is all a secret, remember?"

For a moment Joanie looked exactly like her mother: sad and discouraged and beautiful. It made Masterpiece's heart hurt.

Joanie gave herself a shake and tucked the painting under the others before returning the pile to its home under the bed. "Anyway," she said with deliberate cheerfulness, forcing on a smile, "it's *your* turn for a portrait now. The first thing we need to decide is what sort of pose—oh!"

Masterpiece, a veteran of several portraits, had taken charge, trotting forward to sit in profile with the crate of books behind him, his ears relaxed and his head held high, gazing soulfully into the imaginary distance.

"Wow, Lucky, you're a natural!"

The air filled with the rich tang of shoe polish as Joanie opened tin after tin from her supply box, armed herself with a fresh square of cardboard and a handful of greasy rags, and got to work.

Masterpiece had thought he knew what to expect from being painted. But as Joanie's calm, careful fingers dipped into the tiny pots of shoe polish, he realized this, like the bath, was going to be an entirely new experience.

The artists Count Pulaski had commissioned had all been famous, and they had all been prickly, temperamental people. One had insisted on total silence in the studio or she refused to paint; even birdsong or passing traffic could make her throw down her brushes and put a beach towel over her head. Another had played Mozart operas over and over, humming "Happy Birthday" to himself nonstop and occasionally breaking down weeping. Still another had stopped every fifteen minutes to hurl an egg against the concrete studio wall. None had treated Masterpiece as anything more than a well-behaved bowl of fruit or vase of flowers. None had said a word to him apart from the classic combination of "Sit" and "Stay" and "Quiet."

Joanie, on the other hand, began chatting away happily from the very first smear of polish. It was like her talk during Masterpiece's bath, only this time the subject was her hopes and dreams for her future life. Unsurprisingly, that meant the life she'd seen on TV and in the magazines, with dresses and cars and fancy restaurants.

Masterpiece kept still while Joanie worked, like any well-behaved model, but he let his eyes swivel to check on her from time to time. That was how he noticed there was something odd about the way she painted. Every few minutes she would stop and stare at him with first one eye squeezed shut, then the other.

Joanie noticed him noticing.

"It's my eyes, Lucky," she explained. "They're not the same. My right eye is super sharp, so it does most of the work." She opened it wide, scrunching the left. "I can even read license plates on cars two blocks away! Honest!" She switched. "But my other eye is soft. It never learned to focus after I was born, so everything over here"—she waved an arm to her left—"is always fuzzy. I can see shapes and colors, but no details or edges or anything. I'm used to it, though. I didn't even know it was unusual until we started doing vision checks at school."

Joanie opened both eyes.

"Some people think it's a little strange," she continued. "But it helps me with art! I paint what my soft eye sees, get it? 'Cause everything looks neat all fuzzy, and seeing things two different ways means you have more sides to look at. I think it makes the pictures turn out pretty interesting!"

Masterpiece was honored she trusted him enough to share about her eyes, and even more excited now to see his portrait. He liked the idea that Joanie saw the world differently from everyone else. If that change of perspective helped her create art like this, then a change of perspective seemed like a very good thing indeed. He might even be proving that himself on this unexpected adventure. He certainly was encountering more of the world than he normally saw from behind the window of Poodles, Inc., and it was turning out to be wonderfully refreshing.

When Joanie was done, she cried, "Finished!" and flipped the cardboard around so Masterpiece could see. "What do you think?"

Masterpiece examined his portrait. It was wonderful! Joanie had captured his style and grace, along with the noble angle of his head, all in gentle swirls of white, and gray, and black. He looked tall as a skyscraper, sleek as a limousine, and handsome as a hotel manager. She really was a genius with the shoe polish.

He was a touch surprised to see how little hair he had left, though. He could almost understand Mrs. Dayton mistaking him for a terrier. It was a good thing he still felt just the same inside. After a lifetime of being famous for his dapper appearance, this sudden change would take some getting used to.

He held a paw up toward the painting and wagged his tail hard to show his approval. Joanie beamed.

Just then Mrs. Dayton's voice came drifting down the hall, the outside world pushing its way into their sanctuary. "Joanie! Bedtime! School tomorrow!"

Joanie hastily tucked her painting supplies and the handsome new portrait under the bed, then kissed Masterpiece on the head and disappeared, humming, off to the bathroom. She returned in a threadbare nightgown, her hair brushed and her breath smelling of mint, and climbed under the patchwork blanket with a sigh.

Masterpiece looked around, suddenly uncertain. Where was he going to sleep? He hadn't thought of it before, but there was no bed prepared. No velvet cushion or fleece-lined basket. He blinked up at his friend.

"What are you waiting for?" Joanie patted the blanket. "Come on up!"

Masterpiece's confusion transformed to delight. He had never been invited onto a bed before. Not once in his life. Count Pulaski would have been appalled at the very idea, but Masterpiece had always secretly thought human beds looked like the coziest things in the world.

He jumped up, letting his tail show just how appreciative he was. The mattress turned out to be unexpectedly hard and lumpy, but Joanie made him a nest of blankets beside her pillow, and after walking a dozen turns, Masterpiece curled up, snug and warm and wonderfully happy.

Sleeping on a real bed! It was a dream come true.

Running water and the murmur of grown-up voices drifted through the gap under the door; the sounds of the house settling down for the night. Joanie reached out to click off the light—the room was so small she could do it from her bed—and darkness settled in. To Masterpiece's utter amazement, he felt Joanie's arms go around him, first one, then the other, pulling him close.

Being up on the bed was already a miracle, but he had never even imagined sleeping in a human's arms. It was the most marvelously friendly feeling. He couldn't believe he'd been missing out on this his whole entire life.

One last happy surprise to end a long, sometimes confusing, and overall highly unusual day.

nine
A BAD GUEST

Friday mornings were always busy at the Banbridge Arms Hotel. The usual crowd of business guests needed to be checked out and their rooms turned over quickly before the weekend tourists began rolling in.

Tammy Tonsil could handle busy. She'd been a housekeeper at the Banbridge Arms for thirty-three years this April, and no one could make a neater bed or fold a stack of towels faster. She had the employee recognition awards to prove it.

What Tammy was truly famous for, though, was her unshakable skill at customer service. Everyone on staff agreed she was the queen of cool when it came to difficult guests, and she was often called on to give her coworkers a hand. With her decades of experience, Tammy could resolve even the tensest situation or get the worst-behaved visitor to smile. She had a system.

She practiced her own best smile as she passed a mirror hanging in the fifth-floor hallway. Her red-brown hair— Autumn Delight, according to her latest box of dye—was gathered in a neat bun. Her makeup was, like always, a careful balance between professional and bold. Today that meant raspberry lipstick, coral blush, and a hint of a cat eye with Elizabeth Taylor's own "Midnight Magic" eyeliner, all combining to make her pale, slightly wrinkly face appear fresh and youthful and dynamic. Well, in her eyes, at least. And since that was all that mattered, she gave herself a wink.

She'd only made it a few paces past the mirror when the door of room 514 flew open beside her and a woman exploded into her path.

"What sort of service do you call this?!" shouted the guest, without any attempt at a greeting. "This is supposed to be the finest hotel in this nowhere town!"

Tammy Tonsil peeled herself off the flowery wallpaper, patting her hair and putting a hand to her chest to check that she was still breathing.

She eyed the woman, already positive who she was. Bertie the bellhop had warned Tammy about this guest when she started her shift. Who arrived in the dead of night like that, hammering the check-in bell and demanding their finest room for her and her cat? The woman's powder-blue sedan was still parked improperly out front, taking up two whole spaces. The room was dark behind her, but Tammy could see the flashy red coat the night staff had especially mentioned lying in a heap beside a chair.

Tammy gave a polite nod. "Good morning, Miss Knickerbocker." There had been no way she could forget that name. "I'm sorry if we've disappointed you. Was there something—"

"I was supposed to receive an alarm call!" interrupted Holly Knickerbocker. Her high, trumpetlike voice was impressive. "I have very urgent business to attend to today!"

Tammy flexed both her big toes and made her smile even wider, stage one in her system. "I'm so sorry if you missed your alarm," she said, carefully keeping her own voice soft and gentle. "Though I think you'll find we *did* call you at the time requested, as early as it was."

"Balderdash! Who claims to have called me?"

"Why, I did, Miss Knickerbocker." Tammy pressed her thumbs against her pinkies and imagined a puppy sitting on a pumpkin. That was stage two. "You answered, and you said, 'How did you get this number. Don't you know who I am. Shrimp is out of season. Don't ever call here again, Montgomery Boyd.'"

There was another pause. This one was longer.

"I . . . I don't recall that."

"Of course. That's perfectly understandable. You did get into your room rather late."

Tammy, feeling the encounter shift in her favor, gave Holly Knickerbocker a friendly wink.

Holly Knickerbocker's face turned as red as the crumpled-up jacket.

"Well, since you still failed to actually, properly *wake* me," she declared, "I want breakfast up here in ten minutes." She turned, shouting over her shoulder. "The best you have. With *extra maple syrup!*"

The door slammed, and the sound of someone venting their frustration filtered out into the hall.

Tammy Tonsil stared at the door for a long count of ten, then headed down to the office, humming "Somewhere Over the Rainbow" and wiggling her ears while rolling her tongue. That was stage three for managing stress caused by a difficult customer. And it had been a long, long time since she'd had to use it.

Inside the room, Katerina rolled her eyes as Holly kicked the furniture and ranted about oversleeping and customer service and missed chances with her runaway poodle.

Really, Katerina thought, stretching elegantly on the back of the settee, why did everyone care so much about that boring little animal? True, he was said to be the most valuable dog in the world, but he was still a *dog*. Money was grand, but no amount of money could be worth this much loss of dignity.

The only thing that finally won her interest was the arrival of the breakfast tray, delivered while Holly Knickerbocker was getting herself together in the powder room.

Katerina had overheard Holly's encounter with the housekeeper, so she wasn't surprised when the bellboy slid the tray just inside the room, then ran away, clearly avoiding its inhabitants. She hopped down and glided over.

The meal was covered with a silver dome. Katerina knew how to handle those.

She tipped it easily to one side, made her selection, let the dome fall back, and returned to the settee to enjoy her meal.

Holly would be complaining about the lack of bacon all morning now, but she was always complaining about something.

And if Katerina was going to be stuck in this dreadful low-class town for who knew how long, all for the sake of a dog, then she certainly deserved some compensation.

Ten
A BAD TURN

The sky was blue and the early air brisk as Masterpiece trotted at Joanie's side through the residential streets of Banbridge.

He'd already had the most marvelous morning. He had woken warm and comfortable, sprawled on his back with his legs in the air and Joanie's arms around him. He'd felt so happy, his heart so full, that he had licked her face. That, of course, had woken her up.

After hugging and kissing him until he was nearly worn out, Joanie had jumped up and pulled back the curtain on her little window. Masterpiece had stood to look, more than half expecting his usual view of downtown Manhattan: the crowds, the yellow taxis, the sparkle of shops, the ferocious pigeons of Fifth Avenue. But Joanie's window looked out over the empty lot of oil cans and a stunted-looking pine tree, and he had felt all the strangeness of this new world settle around him, along with a wave of anticipation and excitement. Usually, the count would have a schedule of where Masterpiece had to be, and when. But now . . . he had no idea at all what the coming day would bring. He was on a real adventure!

Morning in the Dayton house was a choppy affair. The grown-ups were already banging around in the kitchen when Masterpiece and Joanie got up, and after Joanie let him out, then in again, Masterpiece settled to watch as Joanie ate cereal and orange juice and Mr. and Mrs. Dayton downed mug after mug of coffee.

When they'd finished, Mrs. Dayton served Masterpiece a bowl of cold onion soup with crackers and cereal mixed in. He was hungry enough not to mind.

After much hurrying in and out of the bathroom, and a great deal of shouting at the clock, all three Daytons hurled themselves out of the house into the morning light. Masterpiece noticed that for all their effort, Mr. and Mrs. Dayton still looked as tired and rumpled as they had the previous night. He imagined it must get just the tiniest bit wearing, shining and repairing shoes day after day after day.

The whole Dayton family started off together, Masterpiece trotting to keep up as they walked across the train tracks, down Nickerson Street, and up Twelfth. At the corner of Park, they parted, Mrs. Dayton reminding Joanie to study hard and come to the shop straight after school. Then Mr. and Mrs. Dayton plodded toward Main Street, and Joanie and Masterpiece continued down Park alone.

Joanie began skipping as soon as her parents were out of sight. She was wearing one of her plain school dresses today—a long, bulky thing in beige and brown—but as she skipped and twirled down the sidewalk, Masterpiece thought she made the dress look almost pretty.

He scampered beside her, delighted to be walking his friend to school. He was relieved, too. Over breakfast the Daytons had debated what to do with him during the day, and Mrs. Dayton had made it clear that leaving him alone in the house and bringing him to the shop were both out, as of course was sending him into Joanie's classroom. For a while it had looked like Masterpiece was going to spend his day tied to the electricity meter outside Joanie's window.

But then Mr. Dayton had recalled how back in his day, lots of kids would bring their pets to school and the dogs would wait for them at the gate. It had been a mark of pride among the kids to have your pet still waiting patiently when the final bell rang.

Joanie had been delighted by the idea, and reluctantly Mrs. Dayton had been persuaded to give the plan a try.

Joanie skipped and Masterpiece trotted as they went along, both of them admiring the fresh-leaved maple trees lining the sidewalk. The houses they passed were small and simple, but all distinctly nicer than the Dayton family's home. Most had neat green lawns and American flags by the door, and some had beds of shrubs and beautiful flowers.

"See that, Lucky?" Joanie said, slowing her walk as they turned onto a side street. She pointed above the trees, to where the top of a tall building was visible several blocks away. "That's my school."

She didn't sound entirely happy to have it so near.

Their path looked like it should lead them right there, but to Masterpiece's surprise, Joanie turned again at the next corner.

"I never go down that part of Maple Street," Joanie explained when Masterpiece cocked his head at her. "That's where the Archer kids live. And the Payton-Prices."

Masterpiece was confused. What could be wrong with meeting other kids? He'd heard stories of kids who bit and yelled and pulled tails, of course. But they were rare. Surely any kids Joanie knew wouldn't be like that.

As if conjured from thin air, a small group of children came into view as Joanie and Masterpiece reached the next intersection. The kids were lounging around a mailbox, and they appeared to have been waiting for something.

"Oh, no," Joanie murmured.

Masterpiece watched with interest as the six children sauntered across the street and right into his and Joanie's way.

Joanie stopped, so Masterpiece sat down beside her. The children were all clean and neatly dressed in shirts and slacks, dresses and bows, which he found familiar and therefore encouraging. One of the girls, who looked to be the oldest, even smelled something like flowers. All the kids were smiling.

Joanie was *not* smiling. She smelled anxious and wasn't making eye contact with any of them. Masterpiece wondered if it was because the children's smiles were showing a few more teeth than was necessary. Among dogs, at least, that many visible teeth could be misinterpreted as threatening.

"What've you got there, *Jokey*?" asked the oldest girl, pointing at Masterpiece. "Did you find a pet rat to be your friend?"

"I think that's some kind of dog, Margo," said one of the boys. His slicked-back blond hair shone in the morning sun. "It sure is ugly, though. And look, it's got mange. Gross!"

Masterpiece gave a start of surprise, making the onion soup slosh in his stomach. Had he heard that right?

"Bet she gets it, too," said another girl. "Mange always spreads to dirty things."

"Not like she could tell if she did," chimed in the shortest boy. "Jokey can't see! She's only got one eye that works!"

And all six of the clean, horrible children squinted one eye and began making faces at Joanie.

Masterpiece was shocked to his core. Why were these children being so cruel to his wonderful friend?

Joanie didn't try to speak up or stop the children. Instead, she stood there quietly, her eyes down, working the toe of one shoe into the sidewalk as the children moved on to her clothes, taking it in turns to mock her dress for being old, patched, and faded.

Masterpiece was so upset, the pads of his paws began to sweat. These children hadn't seen how pretty the dress looked when Joanie danced! And the patches on her dress were neat and even, sewn by Mrs. Dayton's stern, tired, but certainly caring fingers. Couldn't these children tell that Joanie's parents were looking after her the very best they could?

Masterpiece couldn't stand it. He searched his brain for something, anything he could do to help.

Barking and biting jumped to the front of his mind immediately, and he shivered, surprised at himself. He was *not* that sort of dog! Besides, he had never really had practice at either, and with six aggressive children to handle, things might not go his way.

But if he couldn't scare the kids off, then what? All the tricks he knew—and he knew an awful lot—were aimed at pleasing humans, making them laugh and clap and smile. How could any of that help? Unless . . .

The awful kids' faces were all turning red as their bullying barrage continued. Joanie, on the other hand, had gone terribly pale.

Not stopping to think, Masterpiece reared up on his hand legs, raised his forepaws as high as they would go, and began to prance. This trick had made Joanie smile the day before; maybe it would distract these cruel children. Not that they deserved to see it.

All six children stopped shouting and stared, openmouthed, as Masterpiece paraded back and forth. He had their attention!

He was just wondering what to transition into next— maybe a series of backflips?—when the oldest girl pointed at him and gave a high, sharp laugh.

Soon all the children were laughing. They roared and guffawed and slapped their knees, and Masterpiece felt himself deflate a bit. He'd expected his usual cheers and applause. It was hard to maintain the heroic pride of rescuing Joanie while he was being mocked.

"Jokey's dog is as big a joke as she is!" the tall girl shouted.

The others crowed and cackled, and two of them even imitated Masterpiece's prance. But he kept going. His plan was working. They had backed off Joanie. In fact . . .

"All right, this is too wild," the blond boy said, waving a hand. "The bell's gonna ring soon. Let's go."

With a last round of jeers and laughter, the kids moved away in the direction of the school.

Masterpiece lowered to a sit, allowing himself the very tiniest growl at the departing figures. He kept it so quiet there was no chance anyone could hear, but he still felt a little guilty.

He looked up at Joanie, worried he would see her silently crying. But she was smiling down at him.

He met her eyes, and then both of them were smiling. Joanie understood why he'd done his trick; he could tell. She understood, and she was grateful. And Masterpiece discovered that that feeling was even better than applause.

Joanie gave him a very fine curtsy, which Masterpiece returned with a circle spin. Then the two good friends continued on their way.

Joanie's school turned out to be surrounded by a high metal fence, and they made their way around to the entrance gate, where big letters spelled out BANBRIDGE ELEMENTARY. Children of all ages were rushing through the gate, joining their friends around the schoolyard.

"We have to say goodbye now, Lucky," said Joanie, kneeling down. "School gets out at three, if you know when that is, but you don't really have to wait out here for me if you don't want to. It would probably get boring, and someone might report you since people won't know you're my dog."

My dog. Masterpiece liked the sound of those words from Joanie. He felt even closer to her after saving her from those awful kids. They had shared an adventure.

"So, you can go explore the town if you want," Joanie went on. "Just be careful, and meet me back outside the shoe shop before it gets dark. Can you remember your way there? Since we met in the alley? That's something dogs can do, right?"

Masterpiece had never had to find his own way anywhere in his life, but he knew he had the sense of direction all dogs were born with.

"Woof," he said cheerfully.

Joanie kissed Masterpiece on the head, then walked backward into the school lot, waving. A few other kids looked over at him, and some of them pointed, but he kept his eyes on his girl.

His heart gave a pang, partly because it hurt to be separated from Joanie, partly because he was worried about letting her go inside on her own. What if she met those awful rich kids again? What if other kids were mean to her? What if she had no one to speak up and defend her? Masterpiece would certainly get involved if he was there. Maybe that was why dogs weren't allowed in school. No good dog would allow their person to be bullied.

He noticed that all the other children were talking and laughing in groups, but not Joanie. She was walking along by herself. It almost looked like she was trying to make herself small.

What was wrong with all these kids? Why were none of them rushing up to greet her? To say how happy they were to see her? Couldn't any of them see how wonderful Joanie was?

A bell began to clang over the school, and grown-up voices called from the doors. There was a great surge of movement, and all at once the last of the children were disappearing inside.

Masterpiece was alone again. But not like before. He had his girl now, and she would be coming back. She had promised. The next six hours of the day were his, and he was in a strange new town.

It was time to do something he'd never been allowed to do before: head out into the world, and go exploring.

Eleven
A STRANGE TOWN

Masterpiece set off with a bounce in his step, following his instincts and the faint smells pulling him toward Main Street.

Soon the heart of Banbridge stretched out before him: restaurants, clothing stores, hardware and electronics shops, jewelry boutiques and hairdressers. It was nothing like the gleaming skyscrapers of Manhattan, but he liked the stores with their bold, colorful signs. He liked the trees lining the streets. He liked the swish of brooms as store-keepers swept their sidewalks. It looked an awful lot like a film set he had visited once in Hollywood. But this town was splendidly real.

The business nearest Masterpiece was a car mechanic's. A man in a blue jumpsuit was washing a Studebaker station wagon out front, sending swirls of bubbly water sliding over the blacktop. Masterpiece could smell the lemon-edged soap. He sat down to watch as the worker slid a sponge across the windshield, making the view inside warp and waver in the sun. It reminded Masterpiece of *impressionism* and Joanie's paintings, and he remembered what she had said about how her "soft" eye worked. He wondered if this wavy shimmer was the sort of thing she meant. The world wouldn't look too bad like that, he decided. Such graceful softness. Joanie was very lucky.

The worker, an older man with graying hair and a pink, craggy face, looked up and caught sight of Masterpiece. He began to smile, then squinted, thrusting his square face forward. The smile turned to a frown.

Masterpiece, still watching from a polite distance, was not prepared at all as the hose suddenly turned in his direction. The man was spraying water at him! On purpose!

He hopped up only just in time to scamper out of range.

The man kept the cold rain aimed after him as Masterpiece trotted all the way across the street, glancing back over his shoulder in disbelief.

What was *that* about? Had the man been joking? Did he think Masterpiece looked in need of a bath? It seemed like an odd thing to do, whatever the reason, and a very poor joke, if it had been one.

He continued his walk, determined to enjoy himself.

There were humans out and about, strolling in singles and pairs, but he didn't see any other dogs on their own. That was normal. Humans seemed to think unattended dogs were wild beasts who would chew up their shoelaces or rob their banks. Masterpiece himself had never gone walking solo, and while he got a few suspicious looks, he was soon having such a marvelous time he didn't mind.

During all his walks in the past, Count Pulaski had insisted on only the best public behavior from his prize poodle. That had meant staying precisely two feet in front, never greeting other dogs on the street, never jumping or rolling or lying down, and absolutely never running off to follow interesting smells.

But now Masterpiece was taking himself for a walk, which meant he was free to behave however he liked. So, with a nervous, happy squirm in his belly, he gave a little wildness a try. He chased after pigeons, he ran around corners, he ate crumbs off the sidewalk, he investigated smells, and he rolled on his back on the cool morning grass until he laughed and hiccuped and sneezed.

Every moment of it was glorious, better than he'd ever imagined, and for the first time, Masterpiece understood that his walks with the count had never been about what made *him* happy. They had always been about the count.

The count had spent most of their walks giving out

autographs, chatting with friends, showing off Master-piece's tricks, and having a marvelous time. All while he, Masterpiece realized now, spent every minute in public properly behaving. Had the count been making him *work* on their walks all these years? Had he been taking him around town because it was good for business? That was flattering, sort of, but Masterpiece couldn't help feeling that his whole life up till now might have been considerably nicer with just the tiniest bit of freedom. Something Count Pulaski had never once given him.

The realization rattled Masterpiece.

He blinked at the sky for a long moment, then jumped up and got back to exploring his freedom while he had it, racing across the grass and startling three squirrels on the way.

He almost fell over from tail wagging when he found a particularly dog-marked fire hydrant on the corner by the bank. There were other dogs in town! Lots of them! He lost himself in the overlapping notes of *Hello Hi Howdy Hello Hey there Hiya* going back months. It was wonderful read-ing messages up close like this rather than catching hints of them on the air. He had been missing out on so much.

The next block over, Masterpiece found himself outside a brick building with the words BANBRIDGE PUBLIC LIBRARY over the entrance. The door was propped open to the warm spring day, and Masterpiece trotted forward, his nose twitching. He had always loved the smell of books—warm and spicy, sweet and sandy, with just the faintest trace of banana. Breathing deeply, he strode inside.

The library was far smaller than any Masterpiece had visited before. He had attended many charity functions at the Midtown New York Public Library, the one with the big stone lions out front, and that place was almost a cathedral, full of marble and grand staircases and history. This library was more like a weekend bungalow, with simple lines, wood beams, and high, rounded windows.

Masterpiece padded quietly among the shelves, feeling content. He loved the peace of a library, and this one was especially quiet, with only a handful of humans scattered about reading. He walked up and down the rows of bookshelves and tiptoed past the desks, smiling at everything and sniffing whatever he felt like, though being careful not to disturb the readers.

The children's section contained a pile of squashy pillows where two toddlers were playing, waving soft-edged books over their heads. Masterpiece wagged his tail at them as he walked by, and the toddlers immediately began to yell. A purple-hatted woman raced over from the stacks and shushed them, refusing to believe they had seen a real-life doggy.

The librarian, an elderly woman with skin the color of paper and hair dyed a bold, primary red, had been behind the front desk when Masterpiece came in, but as he finished his first circuit of the building, he saw that she had gone. Curious, he wandered behind the desk to see what there was to see. It was fascinating! There were pens and pads of paper; typewriter ribbons and stamps; brads and paper clips and string. Also a box of tissues and a tin of instant coffee, and oh, how *wonderful*: an open packet of cinnamon sugar cookies. Masterpiece's very favorite kind.

He had only just gotten to nosing the wrapping, the luscious scent of cinnamon and butter singing in his nostrils, when the red-haired old lady reappeared.

Then quite a lot began happening all at once.

The librarian's sensible brown shoes lashed out one after the other, and Masterpiece only just dodged them by jumping right up onto the circulation desk. He was shocked all over again! Forget spraying hoses, who *kicked* at dogs? Who would even think of such a thing? No librarian he'd ever heard of, that was for sure!

He had a good view of the library from up there on the desk, and the people in it, startled by the librarian's yell, suddenly had a very good view of him. The toddlers began shrieking and pointing while the purple-hatted woman put a hand over her mouth, and from all around the room grown-ups pointed and yelled. Behind Masterpiece, the librarian raised a rolled-up copy of *National Geographic*, her eyes wide and her wrinkled face furious.

Deciding it was time to make as dignified an exit as he could manage, Masterpiece launched himself off the desk, slipped and squirmed around the feet of an elderly gentleman, and escorted himself at speed back through the open door into the sunshine.

As he resumed his stroll, he pondered the strange people he had met. Why had the mechanic sprayed water at him? Why had the librarian not wanted to share her cinnamon sugar cookies? Why had the sight of an innocent dog standing on the circulation desk caused those people so much concern? Humans were very strange here in New Jersey.

A sudden rumble from his stomach caught him by surprise. Well, he hadn't had the best breakfast, that was for sure, and while he'd had a nibble or two off the street, it was well past his usual morning biscuit hour. In fact, a look at the sun told him it was getting on to lunchtime! There'd been so much to explore, the morning had quite slipped away.

He raised his nose, catching the angle of the wind and sorting through its ribbons of smells. One seemed like exactly what he was looking for, but right as he caught it, the wind shifted and he had to run into the street to follow. A car swerved, its horn blaring, but he barely noticed. He had re-snagged the smell, and it was wonderful beyond belief. It was meat. Lots and lots of meat.

Another block of Main Street slipped by like a dream as Masterpiece wove among people, cars, and lampposts, following the ribbon of scent all the way to the door of Pontowsky's Butcher Shop.

Helpfully, a woman in a fashionable yellow scarf was just leaving, so Masterpiece, putting on his best smile, friendliest eyebrows, and most courteous tail wag, trotted past her high-heeled shoes and into the shop.

Surely the humans in this place would know how to behave, he decided. Not everyone in this little town could be as odd as the ones he'd met. Here at the butcher's he would get some lunch, make some friends, and that would be that.

Things were bound to work out better this time.

Twelve
A SLICE OF PIE

Tammy Tonsil was tired. It had been a long morning, and that awful woman shouting at her about wakeup calls had set a lasting rain cloud over her spirits. She slid into her usual booth at Cathy's Diner with a sigh, hoping an early lunch would lift her mood.

"The usual, dear?" Cathy Muffler called from behind the counter.

Tammy waved and nodded. She looked around at the other regulars enjoying their quiet Friday afternoon, then turned to gaze out the window. Everything seemed peaceful, and Tammy was just starting to feel her mood lift when—Oh, no.

That woman was stalking down Main Street.

Just the sight of her got Tammy's back up. The woman was marching along like her high heels were knives and she was angry at the pavement. Her nose was so high in the air it was a wonder she could see where she was going. And her flashy, expensive outfit was clearly meant to be noticed and envied.

"What's caught your eye there, hon?"

Cathy had arrived, setting a large bowl of clam chowder, two soft rolls, and a slice of lemon meringue pie on the table. Her eyes moved to the red-coated woman across the street. "Hmm. That one a guest at the hotel?"

Tammy pulled her gaze from the window. "Now, Cath, you know I can't go talking about our guests," she said. But she nodded as she unfolded her napkin, making her eyes go wide and her mouth go tight so Cathy would understand.

Cathy's arms, strong from rolling out pies and pummeling bread, crossed over her apron. "Well, I'll watch my step if she comes in here," she said. "From the look in *your* eyes, treasure, she'll be worse than a stack of angry skunks. It takes an awful lot to get to you!"

Tammy was glad she'd been able to warn Cathy about the difficult guest. People who worked directly with the public always had to have each other's backs. Especially when rich outsiders arrived in town.

The bell over the door chimed as Cathy headed back to the counter. Tammy glanced up from her first spoonful of creamy chowder to see Harold Apple entering. For a moment she thought she saw something move down by his feet, but she blinked and there was nothing there, so she decided she must have imagined it.

"Hello, Cathy! Hello, all!" Harold boomed. Harold Apple was the mechanic at the auto shop, and always spoke loudly enough to be heard over a car engine. "Ya read about that missing dog in the paper, Cathy?" he said, settling onto a stool at the counter. "Some sort of celebrity poodle, does all sorts of tricks and worth a bundle!"

"Can't say I did," Cathy replied, pouring him coffee.

"I can't figure what would make a dog worth so danged much," said Harold. "But paper and radio both say to keep an eye out. Big reward, you know! Maybe we'll find the dog ourselves and make our fortune!"

Tammy chuckled along with several other diners.

"Hey now, I did actually see a strange dog earlier," said Harold, smacking a hand to his forehead. "But no, it can't be the same one. This wasn't any show poodle, that's for sure." He imitated a prancing walk from his bar stool. "Besides, this mutt had a bad case of mange. Its coat was all funny looking, hair falling out and all. I had to turn the hose on it just to make it go away!"

Tammy shivered at the thought, then shivered again as something soft brushed her leg under the table. She gave a start, then laughed at herself—it must have been her coat falling off the bench, no need to be silly. She reached down to retrieve it.

Only her groping fingers didn't find her coat, they found . . . fur. Warm fur. She prodded, and the fur disappeared, replaced by a flash of wet as *something licked her hand.*

Tammy barely had time to snatch her arm back before a tiny dog jumped into sight on the bench opposite her. It sat up straight, gazed longingly at Tammy's slice of lemon meringue pie, looked her full in the face, raised both eyebrows, and *smiled.*

Tammy Tonsil did not smile back. She was not a fan of dogs, and definitely not of wild, funny-looking dogs—*was that a SELL BY sticker from the butcher shop on its leg?*—asking to share her lunch.

Tammy stared at the dog. The dog stared at Tammy. Over at the counter, Harold was still gabbing away happily.

No one else in the diner was aware of the situation.

Tammy decided to change that.

"DOG! Dog in the diner!" she hollered, scooching out of the booth so fast she almost left her shoes behind.

Shouts of "Who?" and "What?" and "Did you say *dog?*" went off like popcorn all around her, but it was Harold Apple who dropped his coffee with a clatter and came running to her rescue.

"I'm here, Tammy!" he yelled, leaping past goggling diners. "I've got it!"

Tammy turned to face her booth again, only to find that the dog, seizing its moment, had made short work of her lemon meringue pie. The whipped cream and meringue smeared all over its muzzle now made it look more than a little like a tiny canine Santa.

Harold skidded around the nearest booth, flailing his arms as he arrived. The meringued dog blinked at the sight of him and made as though to jump off the seat.

Unfortunately for him, Harold and Tammy were now blocking every path of escape.

"It's that dog I saw at the garage!" Harold cried. "The one with all the mange! Everybody stay away from him!"

Gasps and cries of horror filled the diner, and with a heroic roar Harold lunged, his suspenders creaking. But he grabbed only air as the animal leapt onto the table, slipped through Tammy's bowl of warm clam chowder, and darted over to the next booth and freedom.

The elderly couple in the next booth had been watching with their burgers held forgotten in front of their mouths. Now they screamed as the little dog pranced across their plates, stepping in the mustard and mayo on the way, Harold in hot pursuit.

The chase continued from one table to another all around

the diner. The dog was clearly only interested in getting away, but as it ran through lunch after lunch, its escape grew more and more sticky and chaotic. At last, with a burst of speed, it doubled back, dodged past Harold, and jumped to the floor.

Paws squelching on the tiles, it made a dash for the exit, but the door was closed, and the dog was forced to start another lap of the diner.

A very crowded chase ensued as Tammy, Cathy, and several other patrons joined in, all trying to help Harold corner the slippery little thing.

"There he goes!"

"You almost got him!"

"Catch him! It could be that missing dog!"

"What are you babbling about?"

"The famous one with a reward!"

"Don't touch it! You'll get mange!"

"Careful! He's coming your way!"

"Just look at him! This mutt isn't worth anything!"

"Get out of my diner!"

It might have gone on all afternoon, but just as the group was rounding the room for the seventh time, the bell over the door dinged. Everyone looked around, and the dog sprinted forward—

—straight into the perfectly dressed form of Daniel Payton-Price.

A burst of frantic and very fancy footwork followed, until, with a *woof* of relief, the little animal got clear, set his sticky paws under him, and vanished down the sidewalk in a blink.

The bell chimed again as the door of Cathy's Diner swung shut, its cheery tone fading into the shocked, echoing silence.

Daniel Payton-Price, the wealthiest man in town and landlord to half its residents, looked down at the meringue, mustard, clam chowder, and who-could-say-what-else smeared across his very expensive shoes and the lower half of his extremely pricey pants.

He looked up, taking in the state of the diner and the red, panting faces of Tammy and Cathy and Harold.

Daniel Payton-Price was known as a man who could keep his emotions under control. But from time to time, it appeared, he understood that it was appropriate to yell.

Tammy secretly thought he could have given the woman in room 514 a run for her money.

Glancing back at her booth and the scattered remains of her calm, peaceful, steadying lunch, she thought she would quite like to join him.

Thirteen
ANOTHER BATH

Masterpiece could not ever remember being so sticky.

His visit to the butcher had ended badly. Butcher shops were for shopping in, it turned out, not eating. Well, it had been an honest mistake to make.

His visit to the diner had at least gone somewhat better—he had eaten, and that pie had been delicious—but the mess plastering his fur, ears, tail, and paws was certainly less than ideal. Why *had* everyone in there reacted so energetically to him? He had only wanted to dine. He'd even sat politely across from his host, the way he'd sat with Count Pulaski almost every afternoon and evening of his life.

He trotted away down Main Street, his paws making sticky sounds on the pavement. A passing cluster of pigeons muttered among themselves, making some very pointed comments about scruffiness, which Masterpiece thought was a bit much coming from pigeons.

Well, his stomach was full, and he still had the afternoon before him. He stopped and sat under a bus stop bench, contemplating his situation. The day was warm, and he could feel his gummy coating of foods beginning to set. He did not want to develop a crust! A bath seemed like an excellent next step.

Masterpiece looked around but couldn't spot any spas from where he sat. So, off he went again, his meringue-flecked muzzle swinging left and right as he searched. More than a few passing humans gave him strange looks, and he even got one decidedly unpleasant scowl before he found what he was looking for: Penelope Hydrangea's Hair & Nail Boutique.

It sounded perfect. He squelched up to the door just in time to slip in behind a tall lady in blue.

Fifteen seconds later he was back out on the street.

Well!

Goodness!

He did a little turn to check that his tail was still there. That woman in the apron had sure known how to use a broom. He'd barely had time to admire the pink-and-yellow interior of her boutique or sniff the chemical flowery smell before she'd descended like a fury and batted him back outside.

He seemed to be all in one piece. But he was still a smeary mess.

He returned to his search, his spirits beginning to feel just the tiniest bit low. What a town this was! He felt a distinct yearning for Joanie and her friendly smile.

The shops of Banbridge passed on either side, none of them useful, until Masterpiece found himself outside Earl's Modern Home, the electronics store where he'd first introduced himself to Joanie. The glowing televisions didn't look quite as impressive in the daytime, but glancing up at them, his interest was suddenly seized fast. *He* was on almost every screen! Picture after picture from his various photo shoots, plus moving footage of him at fashionable events and parties. How strange.

What were all those headlines about? And what did *dognapped* mean?

Some of the screens were showing an interview with Count Pulaski. The man was speaking through tears, wiping at his eyes so his golden rings flashed.

Masterpiece had never observed Count Pulaski from this far outside before. And he realized, as he watched the companion of his life so far, the human who ran and managed every moment of his days, that he did not especially like him.

Oh, Count Pulaski was pleasant, most of the time, but he

did insist on Masterpiece doing what he was told. Even the tiniest slip in Masterpiece's obedience was an absolute crisis in the count's eyes, and Masterpiece was learning he'd missed out on a lot of terribly interesting experiences as a result.

"Call the hotline with any information. Day or night! I am offering a substantial reward!"

Masterpiece's ears were good enough to pick up the count's shouted plea through the windows. A number appeared on the screen, replacing the weeping count.

Masterpiece was confused. What was the count offering a reward for?

All at once, pieces of the puzzle began to come together, and with a shock he realized he might have been wrong about this little adventure from the very start.

Had the lady in the red coat not been a chauffeur working for Count Pulaski? Had she taken him away without permission? Was that what *dognapped* meant? Had he accidentally escaped from a dognapper when he hopped out at that gas station? Was the substantial reward being offered for . . . him?

Goodness, what a to-do!

And as he thought about it, blinking in astonishment there on the street in from of Earl's Modern Home, Masterpiece realized he didn't actually mind that he'd been dognapped. He had gotten to see so many interesting things since, and smell so many interesting smells. And above all, he had met Joanie Dayton. That would never have happened if he'd stayed with Count Pulaski, forever following rules and always behaving exactly as was expected.

The wind changed again, shifting from north to south-southwest, and he caught the lovely scent of moving water. He left the glowing images of himself and Count Pulaski behind and followed his nose, waiting patiently for the crossing lights this time as he moved across Main Street.

Turning the corner at Maple, he found himself outside a beautiful stone-and-brick building surrounded by dignified plants and shrubs. A sign out front announced it was THE BANBRIDGE ARMS HOTEL. Masterpiece's spirits lifted; this was the very sort of place he was accustomed to. Surely he would know the rules well enough to be welcome here.

Best of all, a fountain stood out front, splashing merrily in the afternoon sunshine. It was a bit of a small fountain, as fountains went, but then again he was not a large dog. He sauntered over happily and hopped on in.

Masterpiece thoroughly enjoyed his bath. The water was cool but not cold, the spray was refreshing, and even though he splashed and rolled and rubbed every last scrap of sticky food off himself with help from the fountain's decorative edges, no humans seemed to mind. No one objected, at least, or came running over yelling and lunging like everywhere else he had tried to visit.

There were pennies in the fountain, lots of them, which was a new feature to Masterpiece. They glittered at the bottom like little fish, lending a festive feel to his bathing.

He imagined how Count Pulaski would react if he could see Masterpiece now, and couldn't help letting out a few laughing barks—polite ones, of course—while his wagging tail splashed water over the side.

When he was washed and refreshed and clean all over, Masterpiece jumped down to the grass and gave himself a good shake. It was delightful how well his new short coat shed water. He felt quite sleek and fashionable. Chic! That was the word.

As he pondered what to do next, the double doors of the hotel opened, and a large group of people came out: women and men wearing gray, inconspicuous suits and skirt-blouse combos. Many of them had name tags clipped under their lapels. Businesspeople, Masterpiece decided. He had seen them in hotels around the world, moving together like schools of fish and mostly recognizable by their unfashionable shoes.

Still, these businesspeople were giving him an opportunity to explore, so he trotted over, wove between their feet, and walked right through the open doors of the Banbridge Arms.

The interior was pleasant. It wasn't the Ritz, certainly, but it was clean and formal, and the hotel was obviously run with care. The well-dressed staff were assisting more gray businesspeople in soft, courteous voices; the wood paneling over the front desk shone like burnished honey; and the wine-colored carpets lent the lobby an air of antique elegance.

Best of all, on the far side of the lobby was a window seat decorated with enormous, pale gold cushions. In three shakes, he was across the carpet—unnoticed among the hubbub of departing businesspeople—and leaping up onto the inviting seat.

The cushions turned out to be almost as comfortable as his velvet pillow in the window of Poodles, Inc. He did his customary three turns, arranging the fabric and the stuffing just so with damp paws, and settled down with a happy, comfortable sigh.

His window looked out over a small ornamental lawn. Daffodils ran around the border, and behind them low shrubs hid the hotel parking lot. Masterpiece gazed out, feeling content and peaceful and thinking of a nap, until an unexpected color caught his eye.

There was a gap in the shielding bushes, and through it

one of the parked cars was visible. It was sleek and shining, and it was painted a soft powder blue.

A very *familiar* soft powder blue.

Masterpiece sat up, putting his paws to the glass.

Yes! There was no mistaking that chrome finish and those swooping, expensive curves. That was the very car that had escorted him from Poodles, Inc. The car he'd last seen speeding off without him toward the highway.

A shiver ran all the way from his nose to his tail. The dognapper must be staying right here, at the Banbridge Arms Hotel! She must have come back!

A small, involuntary whine slipped out of Masterpiece as he imagined being dognapped back to the life he'd had before. He would never see Joanie again! He would have to sit and stay and perform and behave whenever Count Pulaski snapped his fingers. And it was sure as sure he'd be kept under lock and key and never allowed even a sliver of a shot at getting away.

The enormous truth struck Masterpiece like thunder: He did not want to go back. Even if this new life was messy, and the people in it could be strange or scary sometimes, he had discovered and experienced so *much* in just one day! And there was still so much more he wanted to do!

He glanced over his shoulder, half expecting to see the lady in the red coat stalking toward him across the lobby. But she wasn't there. Neither were the businesspeople, though. Or any other guests. They were all gone, and the doors were closed. But the lobby was far from empty. The entire hotel staff—the bellhops, porters, managers, and maids—were there instead, a dozen pairs of eyes fixed right on him.

Masterpiece gulped. He had already seen that look on grown-up human faces today. Several times, in fact.

And he had a good idea what it meant.

Fourteen
A FAILURE

Holly Knickerbocker was not having a good day. She had searched up and down this nowhere town, from the alleys and backlots around the gas station to the elementary school dumpsters, from the squalid shoe repair shop to this depressing little city hall.

And there had been no sign of the dog.

The easiest thing would have been to ask around, of course. But that was out of the question. She'd seen that charlatan Pulaski's face on every TV screen at the electronics store. She'd seen the headlines screaming from the front of every newspaper: *Masterpiece Dognapped! Prize Pooch Purloined! Count Offers Substantial Reward!*

That reward, and the fame that went with it, were *hers.* She was not about to give these small-town simpletons the chance to beat her to the prize. One whisper that the dog might be here, and she'd be competing with every one of them.

She glowered at a passing car, making the man in the passenger seat blink in confusion, then spun on her heel, intending to make a sweep of some bushes nearby. Instead, she smashed straight into a couple leaving city hall.

The couple had been chatting together and had not noticed Holly. The resulting crash sent all three of them reeling.

Holly Knickerbocker did not appreciate being crashed into under the best of circumstances—and this was definitely not the best of circumstances. The couple—white, mid-forties, and very put together—were still recovering as she rounded on them.

"Why don't you watch where you're going?" she bellowed. "What kind of people go tearing along sidewalks like that? I could have been killed! I could have broken a heel! Don't you realize these are Chanel?!"

The couple's expressions changed from surprise to outrage.

"For your information," said the woman, pulling herself up and adjusting the hat perched over her twist of chestnut hair, "this dress is also Chanel. And *you* are the one who crashed into *us*! What I want to know is—"

"Oh, I *doubt* that," Holly interrupted. She eyed the

woman's cream-colored dress with as much disdain as she could muster. "That dress is a knockoff. *Maybe.* Who do you think you are?"

The man's face was going splotchy under his slicked-back black hair. "For your information, *ma'am,* I am the mayor of this town. Now, may I ask, who exactly *you* are?"

"Who am *I*? I'm Holly Knickerbocker, you puffed-up nobody, and—" She stopped abruptly. She had not actually meant to reveal that. Searching this town would be a thousand times harder if the locals knew they had a celebrity in their midst.

But it was too late.

"Holly Knickerbocker?" The couple's faces transformed, their snooty scowls blossoming into smiles.

"Holly Knickerbocker! Gee golly, wow!" The man thrust out a hand. "Calvin B. Archer, mayor of Banbridge. It's a real honor to meet you!"

Holly, her own scowl still firmly in place, had no choice but to shake, then do the same with the woman.

"Eileen Archer," the woman gushed. "I am *such* a fan of your columns!"

"We both are," Calvin said eagerly. "So, tell me, what brings a big-city star like you all the way out to our humble burg?"

Holly, so angry she could have kicked herself, racked her

brains for a reasonable lie. They clearly knew her by reputation, so maybe . . . "I'm here to do a piece," she said. "An article. On Dandridge."

"Banbridge," Eileen corrected her with a small cough. "But that is just wonderful news! Isn't that wonderful, Calvin?" She squeezed her husband's arm.

"It sure is, Eileen. It's just swell! And hey, if it's a society piece, you'll sure need our help." Calvin ran a hand over his slicked-back hair. "I'm not one to brag, but I'm not just mayor, I'm also the second-richest man in town." He shook out his jacket sleeve to display a hideously ugly gold watch. Eileen preened beside him, straightening the folds of her supposedly designer dress.

Holly Knickerbocker hadn't suspected it was possible for her to dislike the Archers more, but apparently it was. She wouldn't have given these people the time of day back in New York. She had to get away from them.

"So, what do you think of our town so far?" asked Eileen. "And where are you staying?"

"Why, she'll be staying at the Banbridge Arms, of course!" Calvin answered, before Holly could even open her mouth. "Isn't it just the most fabulous hotel ever? I own it, as a matter of fact! Land, building, and business!"

"I'm sure you're very busy researching your story," said Eileen. "But we would love to help in any way we—Oh!

We were just about to have lunch! Have you eaten?

Holly looked down at her forearm, which was suddenly being pressed by Eileen Archer's hand. She was so stunned at the sheer nerve of the woman she heard herself saying, "No, not yet," before she could think.

Eileen and Calvin parted, re-forming like the jaws of a vise as they each captured an arm.

"Well, then you'll be eating with us," said Eileen. "Our treat, of course!"

"Holly Knickerbocker!" Calvin Archer was shaking his head. "In my very own town! It's marvelous, just marvelous! You'll make us all famous! Say, would you like to hear about our founding and expansion? I've got hundreds of local historical anecdotes."

"It's true, he does!" said Eileen. "Hundreds!"

They marched off, Holly trapped between them with her jaws locked tight, her eyes still sweeping under bushes and parked cars for that dratted dog.

Calvin Archer took a deep breath and began talking.

Holly Knickerbocker fought down the urge to scream. Her bad day had just gotten much, much worse.

Fifteen
A REUNION

Masterpiece was proud to see by the sun that it was just approaching three o'clock as he reached the gates of Banbridge Elementary. He settled down to wait, careful to be in the exact spot where he had said goodbye to Joanie that morning.

His exit from the Banbridge Arms Hotel had been slightly more dignified than his exit from Cathy's Diner and the butcher shop, but not by much. It really was strange being so energetically escorted out of all these buildings by such angry-looking humans.

After the removal, he had strolled until he found a pleasantly soft patch of grass on which to take a nap. It was under a tree, hiding him from passersby, which was convenient. He wasn't worried about the townspeople so much—they were odd, certainly, but only seemed to become agitated when he went *inside* places. He was worried because of that car in the hotel's parking lot. His dognapper was still in town, and almost certainly searching him out.

He had to admit there was a tiny excitement to being pursued. Here he was, living life on the run, with sinister forces on his trail and a substantial reward for his capture. He had accompanied Count Pulaski to enough cinema performances and plays to know a good plot when he saw one, and by everything he'd seen, he was the hero of this one. It was a good feeling, and another new experience to add to all the others.

He did wonder what would happen if Joanie saw the news about him. Did children her age pay attention to those sorts of things? Or read the newspapers? She certainly wouldn't be able to miss it if she walked past the window full of televisions. What would she do when she saw her new friend up there on the screen? What would she think?

He genuinely couldn't imagine.

But he knew what *he* wanted now, at least. He wanted to stay.

At last the school bell sounded its happy peal, and a wave of children came screaming out of the building onto the blacktop. Masterpiece stopped pondering his life and sat up, scanning the crowd for Joanie.

Kid after kid after kid ran by. Kids with shiny shoes and

fancy backpacks, tennis rackets and slide trombones, but none of them were his girl. Finally, his heart leaping, he saw her. She was walking alone just like in the morning, her thumbs tucked under her backpack straps and her eyes on the pavement.

He wanted to run to her, to dance around her feet and prop his paws on her knee so she could scratch his head. But he was a world-class show dog, and he knew how to behave.

Still, he couldn't keep a happy whine from escaping his throat.

Other kids walking by looked at Masterpiece curiously, and some tried to get his attention, clapping their hands or snapping their fingers, but Masterpiece didn't so much as glance at any of them. None of them mattered.

At last Joanie came close enough to spot him, and her face changed completely. Masterpiece thought his tail would fall off from wagging as she flung out her arms and raced over to hug him.

It was a joyous reunion. Somehow the sweetness of it made it seem as though their separation had lasted years, not hours. Masterpiece could not believe how wonderful it felt to be greeted with this much warmth and affection, or how good it felt to give that affection right back. Count Pulaski had certainly never made him feel like this.

His awkward adventures in town, the strange behavior

of the locals, the hose and broom and bellhops and pie—it all faded away as the sight and scent of his friend filled his heart.

"Oh, am I glad to see you," said Joanie, scratching the hard-to-reach spot on Masterpiece's neck and smoothing her fingers over his ears. "This has been the longest day ever. Thank goodness school's out for the weekend."

They set off, and Joanie told Masterpiece all about a spelling test she had flunked, an unfair rule the teacher had made about staring out the window during class, and how Marvin Payton-Price had stolen the dessert off her tray and the lunch lady hadn't done a thing.

Most of what she was saying was a mystery to Masterpiece—he had never spent time around children, and certainly never learned what went on in a school. But he saw that school had made Joanie unhappy, and that was not okay with him. He looked back over his shoulder and, surprising himself, growled at the tall stone building.

Unfortunately, a group of children was walking not far behind. Masterpiece had only a moment to recognize them before the first shout came.

"Hey, one-eye! Your mutt just growled at me!" It was the same pack of awful, well-dressed children from that morning. Masterpiece could feel Joanie tense, but she did not look back.

"Hey! I'm talking to you!" the tallest girl shouted.

"We're gonna call the dogcatcher," the boy with slicked-back blond hair called. "They're gonna lock your dog up and throw away the key!"

Masterpiece did not like the sound of that at all. He was tempted to turn and growl again, but it seemed unlikely to be any help.

Beside him, Joanie sped up. So did the group.

"Hey, Jokey, want to play in our kickball tournament this weekend? Oh wait, you can't! You have to go work at your family's stinky shoe store!"

"Because you're poor!"

"Joke-Joke-Jokey, why you walking so fast? Are you trying to get away from your own smell?"

"Want to stay over at my place tonight? We've got a dog kennel you can sleep in. It's way nicer than your house!"

Masterpiece had thought nothing could shock him after his afternoon, but he had been wrong. How could these children be so mean to Joanie?! She was the kindest, loveliest, most generous human in this entire town! And yet they seemed to take pleasure in tormenting her!

He glanced up, expecting to see Joanie in tears, but her mouth was set in a firm line, her eyes fixed straight ahead. Was this not the first time this had happened, then? Was she somehow used to hearing insults like this? What a horrible thought!

At the next intersection, Joanie turned right onto Holly Street, and to Masterpiece's immense relief the pack of children, growing bored, didn't follow. Soon the last of their jeers faded away.

Masterpiece trotted along, still shaken by the horrible encounter. He wondered what he could do to reassure his girl, to make her smile and feel safe and happy again. But he didn't have to worry. When it was just the two of them, Joanie slowed to a stop, took a deep breath, and exhaled hard, shaking her shoulders and puffing out her cheeks. Then she looked down at Masterpiece and smiled extra wide.

"Hey, do you like flowers, Lucky? This neighborhood has lots of gardens. Come on, I'll show you all my favorites."

Masterpiece did like flowers, but he liked the change in Joanie's demeanor even more. It was like she had simply decided nothing bad had happened. Nothing worth missing out on enjoying her after-school walk, anyway. He felt a powerful wave of admiration for his dear friend. She was so very brave.

So off they went, and Masterpiece never stopped smiling as he and his girl found their own happy, meandering path toward the shoe shop, the rest of the world left far behind, flowers nodding them along every step of the way.

Sixteen
ANOTHER ARGUMENT

Joanie did her best to forget the terrible things the Archer and Payton-Price kids had said as she walked along. She was used to it, of course, after all these years, but this time they'd had a new target in Lucky, and she was surprised how much it hurt when they aimed their words at him.

But that was over for now, and it was wonderful getting to show Lucky all her favorite flowers and trees and gardens, walking slowly like she always did. This stroll to the shoeshine was the best part of her day, and she'd managed to convince her parents that it took a long time to get there from school. Once, a Friday afternoon would have also meant a detour to get three sourballs from the machine outside the drugstore. They were her weekly treat, perfect since she could finish them before she got to the shoeshine, so her parents never knew. But she had given up her allowance for Lucky's dog food. Now there would be no more sourballs until her next birthday. That was okay, though. Having Lucky trotting at her side was worth all the sourballs and nickels in the world.

At last, they reached the very end of Main Street and headed up the steps of Dayton Family Shoeshine. Joanie felt a sudden pang of worry as she turned the handle. Her parents hadn't said if Lucky would be allowed to sit with her in the shop, but she was pretty certain if she asked, the answer would be no.

Only what else was she supposed to do? She wasn't going to send him to wait in that alley and get his coat dirty again. Not after all her hard work. And she couldn't leave him sitting unattended and vulnerable out front. What if the Archer or Payton-Price kids came by? What if they followed through on their threat and called the dogcatcher?

Still uncertain, she opened the door and looked inside.

They had a customer. A man was occupying one of the shoeshine chairs, a newspaper spread in front of him so only his hands and legs were visible.

Joanie's father was perched on a stool at the man's feet, polishing his expensive-looking shoes. He glanced up as Joanie came in, giving her the ghost of a smile, then bowed his head back to his task.

Mrs. Dayton was nowhere to be seen, so Joanie made up

her mind all at once and waved Lucky in after her. He trotted inside, looking around with interest, but Joanie kept waving, ushering him across the floor and behind the counter, where she built a hasty wall of shoeboxes to hide him. Crouching down, she signaled for him to stay still and quiet, and, like the absolute treasure he was, he did.

"Oh, there you are," said Mrs. Dayton, pushing through the curtain from the tiny back room.

Joanie jumped to her feet, hoping she didn't look too guilty.

"Hi, Ma!" she said. "I was just—"

"We received a shoelace delivery today," said her mother, clearly not listening, "and I'm behind on the books. You'll have to wait until your father is done with his customer before you can sweep up, so until then you may as well get a start on your homework." She bustled behind the desk, then shot a sharp look at her daughter. "You left the *you-know-what* outside, correct?"

Joanie gulped twice, then nodded. She felt bad about the lie, but it was too late now.

All at once she wondered how she was going to smuggle Lucky out again when the store closed.

Well, she would just have to sort that out when the time came.

Joanie dropped her bag behind the workbench and

settled into her father's rickety chair. She actually loved sitting back there. Her father had all his tools laid out just so, their wooden handles smooth and burnished from decades of patient work. Paul Dayton was a quiet man, not really given to sharing much about himself with anyone, including his daughter, but sitting back there in his place, she felt like she could understand him a little.

She opened her bag for her workbook, then glanced up as the man in the chair shook out his newspaper, revealing his face. It was the mayor, Calvin B. Archer. His slicked-back black hair shone, and his trademark gold watch glittered under the store's lights. Just by being there, he made the Dayton family business appear even shabbier than usual.

Joanie fought the urge to glare. Did he know the kinds of things his awful children said to her day after day? He should have been a more attentive father. He should have raised them better.

Calvin B. Archer coughed—making no effort to cover his mouth, Joanie saw—and flipped through the paper before settling back down to reading. The front page was visible now, headlines blaring in their oversized type.

Joanie had already begun to turn back to her work, but a particular line of words at the top of the page snagged her attention like a fish on a hook.

PRIZE POOCH STOLEN! SEVEN-STATE SEARCH FOR

"MASTERPIECE"! COUNT OFFERS BIG REWARD!

Something icy seemed to sidle down between Joanie's shoulder blades.

There were pictures under the headline, and thanks to her sharp eye she could see them all clearly. One was of a balding man crying into a handkerchief, his hands covered in rings. The next showed a building called Poodles, Inc., with police surrounding the door to hold back a crowd. A third showed a glamorous, moodily lit portrait of a dog.

A small gray dog.

A small gray dog who should not have looked that familiar.

Joanie was on her feet and out from behind the counter before she realized it, her head spinning like a ladybug caught in a hurricane.

She glanced toward her mother, but Mrs. Dayton was frowning over the ledger and hadn't noticed a thing. Joanie slid one foot in front of the other, avoiding the squeakier floorboards, inching toward the newspaper floating above her father's bent back. She was just close enough to read the caption under the dog's portrait when the door of the shop flew open.

The paper flopped down, hiding the story, as the mayor and all the Daytons turned to look. Joanie had to fight down another glare at the sight of the man walking in.

"Daniel Payton-Price!" Mayor Archer cried, a smile splitting his face. "How the heck are you?"

Banbridge's biggest landlord let the door slam behind him before giving a curt nod to the man in the chair. "Afternoon, Calvin." He completely ignored the Daytons.

"Glad I ran into you, actually," said the mayor. "Big news! There's this reporter woman in town, Holly Knickerbocker, society bigwig from the city, and she's doing a piece on Banbridge! Eileen and I had lunch with her today and let me tell you, she is something! If her article lands right, we could see a major boost in tourism and start making some real money. You've heard of Holly, right?"

Daniel Payton-Price gave a chilly smile. "I'm sure my wife has," he said. "And if you think there's money in it, I can always find time for a lunch."

Calvin Archer grinned and tapped the side of his nose. "Hey, speaking of, what about this poodle business, huh?" He held up his paper. "You see it?"

"I saw. Load of nonsense. No dog is worth that kind of dough."

"Oh, agreed, agreed. And doesn't that count *sell* poodles anyway? Why not just pick himself another dog? Can't be any difference between them!"

Daniel Payton-Price frowned. "Actually, there was a stray dog causing trouble along Main Street today. That's why I'm here." Ha raised one foot, then the other, displaying a sticky mess across his expensive leather shoes. "Little monster got inside Cathy's Diner and was frightening customers. Harold Apple chased it out, but not before it ran into me. Harold said he saw it earlier prowling outside his garage, too, and folks at the library and butcher shop had similar complaints when I stopped by."

Mayor Archer whistled. "The same dog?"

"Sounds like." Daniel Payton-Price cracked his knuckles. "I better not see it again—that's all I can say."

"I hope my girl Margo doesn't find it!" laughed the mayor. "She's always begging for a dog, but she's going to have to get her grades up if she ever wants that to happen."

All at once Joanie realized she was still standing right out in the open. She glanced around in time to see her parents share a meaningful look, then turn to her. She could almost hear them processing the news of an unknown dog running wild across town. She gulped. They had to be thinking it was Lucky.

But that was so unfair! Lucky couldn't have caused all that trouble. No way.

On top of everything, Joanie's brain was still spinning from that picture in the newspaper. Was there a chance Lucky had something to do with the famous missing dog?

Was that even possible? Or was she just seeing connections where they didn't exist, inventing a grand version of her life like her mother always complained she did?

Mrs. Dayton made a face, glanced worriedly at the chatting men, then waved at Joanie to get back behind the workbench. Joanie didn't have to be asked twice.

She did feel a small flare of anger at the rudeness of their customers, though. Calvin Archer didn't seem to have noticed that he was resting his paper right on top of her father's balding head. If it had been Joanie, she would have said something, but quiet, gentle Paul Dayton just kept on shining the man's shoes.

As for Daniel Payton-Price, he still hadn't acknowledged that anyone but his friend the mayor was even in the room. The Daytons might as well have been shoe trees.

Joanie had nearly reached the desk when her mother, turning a page of the ledger, fumbled her pen. It bounced and clattered, rolling for the edge, and Mrs. Dayton lunged to catch it, steadying herself with a foot thrust under the counter. A sudden, high-pitched yelp rang through the shop, and in a shower of shoeboxes, Lucky burst out of hiding and darted wildly across the floor, looking extremely startled.

Joanie knelt without thinking, and the little dog zoomed into the safety of her outstretched arms.

She stood, clutching him tight and bracing for her mother's anger, but Daniel Payton-Price got there first.

"Hey! Hey—that's the dog!" he yelled, stabbing a finger at Joanie. "The mutt I was telling you about! The one that caused all the trouble!"

Calvin Archer's mouth fell open. "*That* dog? That dog right there?" He surged to his feet, forcing Mr. Dayton to scoot quickly out of his way.

Both rich men looked absolutely furious.

"That beast ruined my shoes!" shouted Daniel Payton-Price.

"And tore up shops and public spaces all across town, by the sound of it!" hollered Mayor Archer.

"And the whole time it belonged to you?" Daniel Payton-Price glowered at the Daytons. "Well, I wish I could say I was surprised."

"Should I fetch the police, Daniel?" asked the mayor. "All that property damage and personal distress has gotta total up to a pretty big fine, not to mention negligent pet owner-ship and—"

"No, please! Please don't!"

Joanie had never heard so much fear in her mother's voice before.

"We're happy to pay any damages my daughter's—" Mrs. Dayton gestured weakly at the dog in Joanie's arms.

"—might have caused. And of course, we'll do all the repairs and cleaning, so your shoes are like new."

Mr. Dayton nodded from his shoeshine stool, his hands twisting together. "Like new!" he agreed. "No charge!"

But Daniel Payton-Price was shaking his head. "Oh no, no, no, no," he said. "No, I am *never* bringing my business here again. This is just what I was saying last week, Calvin, about grimy little shops like this one dragging down the tone of our whole town. No, this is the last time I'll ever set foot in here, and that goes for my wife as well. And double for all our friends!"

"Very good!" declared Mayor Archer. His gold watch flashed as he waved his hands. "How can anyone expect clean shoes and proper service from a family that keeps a mangy, destructive animal like that as a pet, anyway? I want it gone, you hear me? And I'll be using every power of my office to make sure no one crosses your door until every penny of damage that animal caused is paid back! With interest!"

"With interest!" shouted Daniel Payton-Price. He turned on his heel and wrenched the door open. "Come on, Calvin. I don't want to waste one more second in this place."

Letting his newspaper scatter across the floor, the mayor stepped down from the shoeshine stand, swept his hat onto his head, and clapped his friend on the back. Heads held high and eyes blazing, the two men left, leaving the door hanging open behind them and a terrible, ringing silence in their wake.

The little dog trembled in Joanie's arms.

It was still early, barely past four o'clock, but as Mr. Dayton crossed to shut the door, he flipped the hanging sign from OPEN to CLOSED. His hands shook as he lowered the shades over the windows, then turned to face his family.

Mrs. Dayton was standing frozen behind the desk. Her face was very white.

"A boycott," she whispered.

"A boycott," said Mr. Dayton.

Joanie looked back and forth between them. Lucky gave her chin the briefest lick and squirmed, but she didn't dare put him down. Not yet.

The two most powerful men in town had just announced her family would be held accountable for whatever had happened downtown. And announced a boycott of their shop. All because they'd seen Lucky. All because she'd brought him inside.

Mrs. Dayton rounded on her. "Joanne. Louise. Dayton. What were you thinking?! Why would you let that dog run loose? And then bring it right inside our store?"

Joanie opened her mouth to protest, then remembered

what her mother had said about "just one problem and he's gone." Trying to explain herself might seem like talking back, and after the mayor and Mr. Payton-Price, she didn't want to give her mother any more reason to be angry.

Instead, she hung her head, burying her face in Lucky's fur as her mother launched into a lecture. She sniffed, fighting back tears, then blinked. Her pup actually did smell like lemon meringue pie. And was that vegetable soup? And . . . copper pennies? What *had* he gotten up to while she was at school?

At last Mrs. Dayton's tirade wound down, and Joanie heard her father clear his throat.

"Sylvia, dear," he said, "I know it looks bad, but I don't think it's fair to ask Joanie to give up her new friend after just one—"

"Did I *say* I want her to give up her friend?" interrupted Mrs. Dayton.

Joanie's head shot up. She shared a look of utter confusion with her father.

"But—but the mayor said—"

"I heard what that man said!" Mrs. Dayton snapped. "And he might run this town, but I refuse to let him dictate what goes on in my family! If anyone is going to make decisions regarding my daughter, it will be me, not Mayor Archer *or* Daniel Payton-Price and his ugly, overpriced shoes!"

Mr. Dayton and Joanie stared at her, both their mouths hanging open. Joanie had never heard her mother speak this way about anyone. Ever. She couldn't help feeling more than a little proud.

Mrs. Dayton finally noticed the effect her words were having on the two of them. For half a second Joanie thought she was about to smile. Instead, she gave a sigh that sounded drawn from the creaky floorboards at her feet.

"Yes, well then," Mrs. Dayton said. "If we're not staying open, we may as well go. Joanie, you can come in early tomorrow and clean up before the store opens. Leave your homework here; you can finish it after."

Joanie nodded in acceptance, then shifted her grip on Lucky, daring to ask, "And what about . . . ?"

"Your father and I will discuss everything else tonight."

Mr. and Mrs. Dayton shared a long, complicated look. Joanie wished she could decode it.

Slowly, the three of them gathered their things, and with Joanie still carrying the newest member of the family in her arms, switched off the lights, locked the door behind them, and set out together on the long walk home.

Seventeen
A REVELATION

Mrs. Dayton marched in front on their walk home, her hands pressing new creases into her dress, her shoes catching on cracks in the sidewalk. Behind her came Mr. Dayton, head bowed, looking like he was being swallowed by his own jacket and shirt.

Joanie brought up the rear, Masterpiece now trotting along at her side. He had left the excitement of the shoe shop behind him and was very much looking forward to dinner, and snuggling up with Joanie for the night, and whatever adventures the next day might bring. There would be no school, which was a grand start. It should mean he and Joanie could spend every single minute together.

He kept one eye on his girl as he walked. All three of the Daytons seemed lost in their own worlds, but Joanie looked as though what she found there hurt her. She looked like someone with a stomachache, a headache, and a tooth-ache all at once. When Count Pulaski had looked like that, he would play sad songs on the gramophone and dance by himself around the ballroom.

The Daytons did not have a gramophone. Or a ballroom. Masterpiece would have to find some other way to cheer her up. Seeing his girl like this made his heart hurt.

At last, they reached the end of Nickerson Street and their little family home.

Masterpiece wagged his tail as the smells of the house—familiar now—swirled around him. He headed to Joanie's room to visit his water dish.

When he returned, Mrs. Dayton was briskly handing out chores. They may have arrived home hours early, but it was clear she didn't think that was any reason not to keep working hard through the afternoon.

With no chores of his own, Masterpiece found a reason-ably warm corner near the kitchen and settled down, ready for another nap. It had been a truly exciting day.

He must have been even sleepier than he thought, because when he woke, there was darkness in the win-dows and he heard the clatter of dishes being done in the kitchen. It seemed the Daytons had already finished their dinner. He got to his feet and stretched, his stomach gurgling.

"Dog's up!" called Mr. Dayton, unfolding his paper at the table as Masterpiece padded in.

"Feed him, please, Joanie," said Mrs. Dayton. "The cans I got are in the pantry."

Masterpiece waited in his corner while Joanie fetched his bowl. What would she serve tonight? From the sound of it, Mrs. Dayton had bought him something special.

When Joanie brought the bowl over, he saw to his great surprise it had been filled with a cylinder of moist, brown, sticky-looking splodge.

Masterpiece sniffed at it. This was his dinner? It smelled like . . . well, he wasn't sure what. *Chicken a la king,* a bit. *Veal en croute.* Perhaps just slightly like salmon mousse. But it also smelled of leather, wet leaves, and sour corn-meal. Very cautiously, he took a tiny bite.

Fifteen seconds later, he was looking down at the empty bowl.

What had just happened? How had that unappealing lump, still marked with ridges from its time in a can, turned out to be one of the most delicious things Masterpiece had ever tasted?

He realized he was licking the bottom of the bowl.

A satisfied grunt sounded from overhead, and he looked up to see Mrs. Dayton and Joanie watching.

"Well, at least he appreciates it," Mrs. Dayton said.

Joanie laughed and leaned down to hug Masterpiece, but something about her still seemed distracted, like she was trying to untangle a difficult problem in her mind.

She took his bowl away to wash and refill with water. When she came back, she gave him a long stare, her eyebrows crinkling together.

"Hey, Pa?" she asked, not looking around. "Can I borrow the paper? Just the front?"

Mr. Dayton blinked in surprise, but he handed over the crinkled pages. Joanie tucked them under her arm and signaled for Masterpiece to follow her to her room.

Joanie set the water dish in its usual spot, then tossed the newspaper onto her bed and settled beside it, looking down at Masterpiece.

"I'm glad you liked your dinner," she said. "And I'm sorry about what happened at the shop. Only, can I just—" She stopped, chewing her bottom lip. "Will you—" She switched to her top lip, apparently needing time to gather her thoughts.

"I just need to check something," Joanie said at last, pressing the tips of her fingers together. "And then I'll know. Obviously, you're the smartest, best dog in the world, Lucky. So can you *sit* for me, please?"

Masterpiece moved into a polite sit.

"Can you lie down?"

Masterpiece lay down, resting his head on his paws.

"How about roll over, please?"

Masterpiece did three perfect rolls one way, then back to where he'd started.

Joanie swallowed hard. "I already know this one, but can you stand?"

Masterpiece was up on his back legs in a blink. He was having fun! It had been a while since he'd gotten to show off like this. Only why wasn't Joanie smiling? She had practically jumped for joy when he did this trick the night before. She had clapped!

True, she *had* thought he was a stray cat at the time.

"Do you know any other tricks?" Joanie asked. "Any at all?"

Masterpiece was starting to feel decidedly confused. But he was happy to do anything for Joanie, so he launched into his full cocktail party routine. He did trick after trick after trick, including the one with the front pawstand tango, which had won him a standing ovation at the opening night soiree for the Helsinki Olympics the previous summer.

When the routine was finished, he returned to a sit, happy and invigorated. It felt remarkably different doing tricks after being invited to, rather than ordered; performing not to impress Count Pulaski's fancy human pals, but to make his own dear friend happy.

Only Joanie wasn't smiling up there on the bed, let alone clapping. She was biting at her fingernails. He had never seen her do that before.

He rose and put his forepaws on her knees, sniffing at her chin to show how concerned he was.

That finally got a smile. Joanie opened her arms, and Masterpiece hopped up onto her lap and turned around three times to settle.

"The thing is, Lucky," Joanie said, rubbing his ears, "I just don't know . . ."

She spread out the paper, the headlines blaring across her patchwork quilt, and ran a finger over the portrait of the missing dog. Her lip went between her teeth again as she studied the picture, first using just her right eye, then her left.

She looked down at Masterpiece and repeated the process. He waited, finally understanding what had been worrying her. She was figuring out the truth.

He could almost hear her piecing it together: His sudden arrival in town, his haircut before she trimmed off all his fur, his party trick routine.

But what difference would knowing the truth make? The fact that he was famous might be confusing for Joanie, but it didn't change how he felt about her.

If only he could tell her that! Joanie still smelled worried.

She puffed out her cheeks, letting out a breath as she lay back on the crinkling newspaper. Masterpiece snuggled close, and Joanie began running a hand along his back.

They stayed like that for a long time. Masterpiece could hear Mr. and Mrs. Dayton talking down the hall, but Joanie remained silent beside him. He knew her well enough by now to know that she was thinking hard about what her discovery might mean. Thinking and thinking and thinking.

He closed his eyes, wishing he could make her understand: He had already made his choice. She was his girl, and he was staying put. And nobody, not Count Pulaski, not the newspapers, not the dognapper lady in red, could ever separate them again.

Eighteen
A PHONE CALL

Joanie was still thinking when her father came in, asked for his newspaper back, and told her it was time to get ready for bed.

She changed into pajamas and brushed her teeth, then returned to her blankets, switched off the light, and snuggled up beside Lucky. He was already snoring softly.

Lucky. Her brand-new, wonderful, funny best friend. Could he actually be this famous missing dog? As strange as it seemed, she thought he must be. His expression in that portrait had convinced her. His adorable little eyebrows and that tilt of the head.

But what now? Should she tell someone? Should she tell her parents? There was no question they would make her give him up if she did. Lucky belonged to someone else, someone who was looking for him, and her mom would have strong feelings about that. She tried to imagine saying goodbye to the little dog, kissing him on the head and watching him disappear down the road in the back of a big, shiny car. Her mind flinched away from the thought.

But if she didn't tell, and no one figured it out, and she got to keep Lucky . . . well, was that right? What if he actually wanted to be found and taken home? Most lost dogs probably did. Would he be happier going back to Count Whatshisname than staying here? Was there any way to check?

Lucky *seemed* happy. But what if he was always like that? What if he didn't have any way to tell her how much he missed being in New York City?

And then there was Mayor Archer's demand that they pay everyone back for the damage the dog had done. Could her parents even afford to do that? Would Mayor Archer keep the boycott going until she sent Lucky away?

Moonlight snuck in past the curtain, illuminating the magazine cutouts taped across her walls. She rolled over, turning her back on them. Usually she loved her collection, but tonight the sight of it made her feel something uncomfortably close to ashamed.

Lucky was from that world. He was used to extravagant celebrities, fine dining and photo shoots, fancy cars and airplane rides. Imagine what he must have been thinking as she'd proudly shown off her bedroom, those taped-up pictures, and her small, cramped house. And the food! They'd fed the world's most valuable dog *oatmeal* and *peas* and the cheapest canned dog food they could find.

Picturing how someone from the world on her walls would see *her* life filled Joanie with an unhappy ache. It made her feel silly and small.

She lay in the dark, her mind churning as the minutes ticked by, sleep a very long way off.

At last, she got up and went to get a glass of milk from the kitchen.

The cold hall floor creaked under her bare feet. She could hear the refrigerator motor hum. A strip of light gleamed from under her parents' door, along with the murmur of voices. It looked like they were still up, too.

Pulled by something she couldn't quite understand, Joanie tiptoed over and put a careful ear to the door.

"—run around like some kind of monster," said her mother's voice. "We never should have let her get attached to that stray."

Joanie felt a chill prickle the back of her neck. They were talking about Lucky.

"And I am terrified, Paul," Mrs. Dayton continued. "Paying for the damage that dog did today is going to really hurt us. We've already burned through our savings. And if the mayor actually does start a boycott, I don't see how our business can survive. I don't see how we can even pay next month's rent!"

The cold feeling slid inside Joanie's bones. She knew her family was poor, but she'd never imagined they were this close to losing everything.

"I don't know what we can do." Her father's voice was low and weary. "At this point, only a miracle could change things. But that's why I think we should let Joanie keep him. With her allowance covering his food, it won't make much difference one way or the other, and none of this is her fault. Why not let her be happy?"

"Because that dog is out of control! Do you want him to go on another rampage? We already owe more than we can pay."

Mr. Dayton sighed. "I'll talk to Joanie about keeping him tied up when she's at school." There was a heavy pause. "Maybe you're right. Maybe letting go of the dog will be how this ends. But right now, Joanie obviously loves him, and we can't ask her to give that up. Not yet."

Joanie pulled her ear from the door, her parents' argument fading to a murmur.

What she'd heard rattled like broken glass in her brain.

Her parents were going into debt, and Dayton Family Shoeshine still might not survive. They might not even be able to pay their rent. All because of Lucky.

And only a miracle could help.

Joanie shivered with the realization that she knew just where to find one. Count Pulaski was offering a substantial reward for the return of his missing dog; a reward like that should be more than enough. She could save everything, save the shop, save their future. She could give her parents peace of mind after all their hard work and worry.

But only if she gave up Lucky.

Her skin tingled. She had never had a feeling like this, not once in her ten whole years. Standing there, alone in the hall in her dark, quiet house, she felt . . . old.

She let herself sob, once, quietly, in the dark. Then she wiped the tears from her cheeks and made her way to the kitchen, her stomach knotting at the sight of the newspaper lying folded on the table.

She took it and slowly crossed to the telephone.

She picked it up.

She unfolded the paper, willing her hands to stop shaking, and dialed the number on the front page.

As the phone rang, she realized that for this one wild, terrifying moment she was tremendously important. She was the only person in the whole world who knew where the missing poodle was. She knew more than all those journalists and investigators and fancy crying rich people. She was stepping into the world on her walls. She was reaching out. And they would hear what she had to say. Even if just this once.

The ringing stopped, and a curt voice greeted her on the other end of the line.

"Hello," Joanie whispered. The word came out rough around the lump in her throat. Everything felt unreal, like she was stuck in a terrible dream. "I—I have a tip to report. I know where you can find him. That missing dog. Masterpiece."

Nineteen
A LUCKY BREAK

"GOOD MORNING, MISS KNICKERBOCKER! THIS IS YOUR ALARM CALL!"

Holly Knickerbocker held the phone out at arm's length and glared at it through eyes still squinted shut from sleep. "Wh-what? Who is this?"

"THIS IS THE FRONT DESK, MISS KNICKER-BOCKER," shouted the cheery voice on the other end of the line. "GIVING YOU YOUR REQUESTED EARLY ALARM CALL THIS FINE SATURDAY MORNING. I DO HOPE IT'S COMING THROUGH LOUD AND CLEAR."

Holly sat up, taking in the light coming in around her room's ugly curtains. "Oh," she said. "Right. Yes."

"WONDERFUL! WELL, FROM ALL OF US HERE AT THE BANBRIDGE ARMS HOTEL, HAVE A MARVELOUS,

SPECIAL, SUNNY DAY!" There was a click, then the dull whine of a dial tone.

Holly slammed the phone on the receiver and flopped back onto her pillows, cursing under her breath. Katerina, who was washing her tail on the foot of the bed, looked over without much sympathy.

"That wretched old maid," Holly grumbled to the cat. "She sounded positively *gleeful* to be shouting in my ear."

Katerina went back to her washing, wondering why humans made up so many pointless words for feelings. *Gleeful.* What was that even supposed to mean? There was being asleep, which equaled happiness. There was being awake, which equaled boredom. That was it. What more could anyone possibly need?

Granted, there hadn't been much sleep *or* boredom around the hotel room yesterday. Holly Knickerbocker had come banging back in after only a few hours, complaining about being forced to have lunch with some unlikely locals. She'd insisted on telling Katerina every story she'd had to listen to in detail, complained again all through their mediocre room service dinner, and spent the entire evening scribbling notes about her search on the hotel's complimentary town map, and plotting—out loud, thank you—how she was going to track down that pointless tiny dog.

By the time they'd turned in, Katerina was hoping the

dog had been eaten by a bear just so they could quit the search and go home. They probably had bears in New Jersey.

"Ugh, at least I am actually awake," Holly Knickerbocker muttered, heaving herself back to sitting and rubbing her thumbs into her eyes. "Although I *cannot* spend another day like yesterday. I need a lead on this case. I need some inside information. Good gravy, Katerina, can you imagine if there have already been tips? Or someone's already found him, even?" The idea seemed to terrify Holly. She lunged across the bed, fumbling for her giant purse. "I've got to check with my contact!"

There was a well-protected secret behind Holly Knickerbocker's ability to know everything about everyone, and that secret was a carefully maintained network of informants. Chauffeurs, bartenders, hairdressers, doormen: If they looked after important people in New York City, Holly had their number. She guarded her address book better than the government guarded the gold in Fort Knox.

Katerina moved on to washing her ears as Holly hurriedly looked up a number and dialed. It didn't take long for someone to pick up.

"Charlie!" Holly barked. "It's Holly Knickerbocker. Listen, Charlie, I need to know: Has anyone contacted your man about finding his lost pooch? Anyone come forward claiming they have it? Anyone *reliable*?"

A long, deep chuckle filled the phone line.

"Hello?" said Holly. "Stop that gargling or whatever right now, Charlie. Pull yourself together."

"I'm sorry, my apologies." Charlie still sounded like he was grinning. Katerina could hear him perfectly, thanks to her excellent ears and Holly's longstanding refusal to allow unfamiliar telephones anywhere near her face. "There's just no one like you, Miss Knickerbocker. I don't know how you do it."

Katerina was mildly interested to see a thrill of fear ripple across her companion's features at Charlie's words.

"What?" choked Holly. "What is that supposed to mean? Are you saying someone *has* called in about the dog? Is that what you're telling me?"

"Yes, ma'am. Last night. Only the person who found it won't come to us for some reason, so the count called me in early. We're leaving to pick it up in about ten minutes."

Holly's fear was visibly turning to panic. She clutched the phone so tightly Katerina thought she might crack the plastic. "Listen, Charlie—listen very carefully. Where does Pulaski have you driving him?"

"A small town in Jersey. Bainridge? Or Manbridge? Something like that. I've never heard of it, but I've got it marked on the map. It's a bit of a drive."

"Banbridge. The town is called Banbridge."

There was a whistle. "Now, how on earth could you possibly know that?"

"Never mind how I know," snapped Holly. Katerina could tell her mind was working fast. "What's important is I need to know exactly where Pulaski is supposed to meet the person with his dog. I need specifics, the address. And what time they're meeting!"

There was a pause on the other end of the phone. A long, heavy pause.

"Remember what I know about you and your affairs, Charlie," Holly said into the silence, her voice going artificially light and sweet. "You weren't always just a driver and both of us know it."

"Okay, Miss Knickerbocker, okay," said Charlie. "I remember. Just please don't go causing trouble for my employer."

"Wouldn't dream of it," Holly said. She snatched the pen and paper from her bedside table. "I promise you, Charlie, the only thing I want in this entire world is to get that sweet, dear, missing little dog back into the arms of his owner."

Katerina scratched comfortably at her neck and smirked. It was rare, but from time to time she did have to admire Holly's style.

When the call ended thirty seconds later, Holly Knickerbocker was in a decidedly better mood.

She seized the phone for the third time that morning and dialed zero for the front desk.

"BREAKFAST!" she bellowed as her alarm call enemy picked up. "I WANT BREAKFAST! THE BEST YOU HAVE. WITH BACON THIS TIME! AND, LADY? YOU ARE GONNA SEND ME *ALL* OF THIS HOTEL'S MAPLE SYRUP. DO YOU HEAR ME? EVERY—LAST—DROP!"

Twenty
A LAST WALK

Joanie had never done so many things behind her parents' backs in her life.

She and Lucky—she could not think of him by any other name—were walking together through the streets of Banbridge, making their way toward Dayton Family Shoeshine.

It was very early, and the birds were still singing their morning songs as the rising sun negotiated its way through a covering of gauzy clouds.

Joanie drank in every detail, trying to squeeze as much as she could out of this final morning with her friend. It had been hard getting out of bed so early, especially with Lucky all warm and snuggly beside her, but she wanted to have as much time with him as possible.

Lucky trotted along in front, happy like always out here

in the fresh air. He didn't know it was their last day together. She hadn't told him. She wanted to leave that for as long as she possibly could.

The store opened at ten on Saturdays, so she had arranged to meet Count Pulaski at nine. It was a long drive from Manhattan, but he'd promised he would make it.

It had been a terrifying conversation. The count had a deep, fancy accent—he just *sounded* rich and famous—and he'd spent most of the call alternately sobbing in relief and demanding to know how Joanie had gotten her hands on his dog. A part of her could still barely believe it had happened.

There had been another big reason to get up extra early, of course: Joanie's parents. Getting Lucky out of the house before they saw was essential, or they would have made her leave him behind, tied up out back like she'd heard them saying last night. And trying to talk them out of it, convincing them to let her take Lucky after all the trouble he'd supposedly caused—well, that would have meant spilling the beans about what she was doing. And Joanie did not want to do that.

This was something she was doing for her family. All on her own. And she didn't want the grown-ups involved until it was over.

When her parents did arrive, ready to open the shop and start the day, Joanie would be waiting with the reward money. She could do her explaining then. And maybe, hopefully, finally get to see her mother smile.

Joanie smoothed her hands over her dress, trying to distract herself from thinking about how much losing Lucky was going to hurt.

It was her best dress, the puffy-sleeved evening gown she'd shown Lucky. She'd chosen it so she would look grown-up and sophisticated when she met Count Pulaski. And in case someone there wanted to take her picture.

She'd been looking forward to wearing the dress again, imagining how wonderful it would feel. But she didn't feel wonderful so far. Walking the quiet neighborhood in her puffed sleeves and velvet bow, she mostly felt a little sick.

Being hungry wasn't helping. They'd both had to skip breakfast, since she couldn't afford to make any noise in the kitchen. Back home her stomach had been too full of nervousness to notice, but now that she'd made her getaway, she was feeling distinctly hollow in her middle.

She'd left her parents a note saying she had taken Lucky for his morning walk and would leave him tied up outside the shop while she did her cleaning. It was partly true, at least sort of, but she hoped the untrue parts would be the last lies she'd have to tell for a while.

Joanie was startled from her worry and rumbling belly by the sound of a tingling chime. Looking around, she saw two boys on bikes coming her way down the middle of the street. The boys had sandy-brown hair and matching satchels slung over their shoulders. They were throwing newspapers from their satchels at each house as they passed, one to the left and one to the right, and ringing their bike bells every time they got a direct hit.

The boys spotted Joanie at the same instant and grinned, slowing their bikes so their tires squealed. Joanie groaned. It was Jerry and Michael Archer, one-third of the mean kids who always teased her before and after school. She had forgotten they would be out early doing their paper route.

"Hey, Jokey!" called Michael as the brothers came to a stop on the sidewalk right in front of her. Michael was a year younger than Joanie, but he always acted like they were equals, probably because Jerry, who was Joanie's age, let him. "What are you doing out here? Did you need a break from your smelly house?"

"Yeah," Jerry chimed in. "And why are you wearing that clown outfit? Are you trying out for the circus, Jokey?"

"Heard your dog made a lot of people mad," Michael went on, pointing at Lucky with his chin. "My dad says your parents have to pay everyone back. How are they gonna do that? Your house isn't even worth as much as my bike!"

The boys laughed.

Joanie raised her head. She'd been trying to ignore the

boys like usual, even though their comments about her favorite dress had hurt, but the reminder about her parents was too much. How dare these mean boys ruin her and Lucky's last morning?

She put her hands on her hips, ready to tell them just how mean they were, but Lucky, trotting forward, got there first.

"Ha ha, is your dog going to dance again?" Jerry said, guffawing. "You two really do belong in the circus!"

But Lucky didn't stand and prance like he had the day before. He didn't growl either. Instead, he walked calmly up to the front wheel of Michael Archer's bicycle, lifted one leg, and peed.

"Ew!" yelled Michael, tugging his bike away. Both brothers backed off.

It was Joanie's turn to laugh.

"Gross!" Jerry shouted. "You and your dog are *gross!*"

"Don't even think about coming back this way later," spat Michael. "If we see you or your dog at our kickball tournament, all our friends are coming after you!"

Lucky put his leg down and calmly began walking toward the boys again.

"Come on," said Jerry, wobbling his bike over the grass verge onto the street. Michael glowered, doing the same, and the boys rode off, shouting insults over their shoulders.

Lucky trotted proudly back to Joanie, who swooped down to kiss the top of his head over and over. It had been a marvelous defense. Although inside she felt a curl of worry. Things would be harder for her now, once Lucky was gone. The Archer brothers would never forget this. And after today she would be alone.

Well, at least she'd have this wonderful memory to smile over. Her final walk with Lucky was turning out to be perfect, after all.

Twenty-One
AN EXPLANATION

At last, Joanie and Lucky reached the shop. The town was coming to life now. One car in particular caught Joanie's eye: a powder-blue sedan parked across the street from the shoeshine. It was so beautiful! She wished she had a shoe polish that color to use in her paintings. She almost pointed the car out to Lucky, but he was busy checking the doggy news at a lamppost, and she didn't want to interrupt him.

Joanie usually liked her solo cleaning time on Saturday mornings. There was a pleasant kind of silence to the empty shop. She felt safe in it, and loved that she could sing or dance if she wanted while she cleaned.

This morning, though, things felt different from the moment they stepped inside. The echo of the hard words from the day before hung in the air, and Mayor Archer's newspaper was still spilled across the floor where he'd dropped it. Almost like a threat.

The clock behind the desk showed it was seven minutes past eight. Joanie swallowed hard. The store opened at ten, and she had arranged to meet Count Pulaski out front at nine. That meant he was already on his way, his car rumbling along the road from Manhattan.

It also meant she had less than an hour left to spend with Lucky. She would have to do her cleaning quickly. She still needed time to explain things to her little friend.

And to say goodbye.

The clock ticked, and Joanie got to work, sweeping the floor, hauling trash through the back door to the alley, scrubbing the windows with vinegar and crumpled pages of Mayor Archer's newspaper.

The clock kept ticking. Joanie dusted the shelves of shoelaces, straightened her father's tools, brushed flies off the windowsills, and polished the arms of the shoeshine chairs.

Lucky sat on the stool behind the counter, watching her, his tail giving an occasional wag of support.

Joanie worked and worked, and at last, all the cleaning was done and the store was ready.

The clock ticked. Joanie checked it.

It was ten minutes to nine.

The old feeling of heaviness settled over her, weighing down her arms and legs like concrete. She returned the brush and dustpan to the back room and paused, giving herself a moment. She didn't want to do what she had to do next. She breathed in the dusty air of the dim storage area, feeling her heart thumping in her chest.

Lucky looked up when she returned, his ears perked, his little tail waving.

She took him in her arms and crossed the tidy shop to sit in the nicer of the two shoeshine chairs. She often did this if she had a spare minute at the end of her cleaning time. The chairs were set high so her father could reach the customer's shoes, and it felt different sitting up there, almost like a throne. Joanie liked that.

She ran a hand down Lucky's back. He gave a happy sigh and rested his chin on her shoulder. Joanie felt tears prickle behind her eyes. She took a deep breath.

"Lucky, I have something to tell you."

She started with her family. She told him how they were poor, despite both her parents working hard to build the shoeshine business and keep it running all these years. She explained how Mayor Archer was promising a boycott until the Daytons paid back everyone in town who thought Lucky had done damage. She didn't want him to feel bad about that, and explained how unfair it was, but it was part of the story and it had to be said.

Finally, she couldn't put off the hardest news any longer.

"And the thing is, Lucky . . . I know who you are now. Your real name is Masterpiece. You're famous. And your owner says you're missing."

The dog's head had shot up at the sound of his real name. He leaned in and licked her chin, then gazed into her eyes. It was like he was trying to tell her something.

"And see," Joanie went on, forcing herself to speak the words, to do the right thing. "The thing is, I . . . I have to give you back."

Lucky pulled away, sitting up tall in her lap. He tapped a paw against her chest and barked once, loudly.

"I know!" Joanie said, reaching out to wrap her arms around him. "I know! I love you, too! But Count Pulaski is your *owner*. Your person. He has to be missing you, and I can't keep you for myself when I know the truth. It wouldn't be right."

It had been hard to start speaking, but now it felt impossible to stop. Lucky began blinking rapidly, making soft whining noises. She had to tell him everything about why she was making this decision. She had to explain.

"And see, my family is poor, like I said. I heard my parents talking last night, and it sounds like things have been bad for a while. If we don't get help soon, we're probably going to lose everything. Especially with the boycott. And the count is offering a big reward for whoever finds you . . . and, well . . . we really need the money . . ."

She felt awful telling him that. It made her feel hollow inside, a thousand times worse than the empty feeling from skipping breakfast.

"It's not like I love you less than my parents, Lucky," she said, tears falling from her eyes as she leaned in to kiss the top of his head. "It's just that they're my family. And if I let you go, I can take care of them better, and you'll be back with your proper owner, and everything will be all right."

Her voice cracked as she finished the sentence. She knew that last part was a lie. She wouldn't be all right. She would be heartbroken for a long time over this. She was losing the only best friend she'd ever had.

A sudden flurry of activity out on the street drew Joanie's eye. From her throne, she had a view through the little window at the top of the door, and she could see people on the sidewalk stopping and pointing, and cars slowing down on Main Street.

Then a very particular car came into sight: a shiny, long, black limousine. It slowed, turning like a shark moving through the deep, and pulled up right in front of Dayton Family Shoeshine.

Joanie looked over at the clock.

The big hand was on the twelve and the small hand was on the nine.

Her time was up.

Twenty-Two
AN ARRIVAL

Count Pulaski yawned.

He had been feeling increasingly weary as his limo drove deeper and deeper into the wilds of New Jersey. Any proper city had been left behind almost an hour ago, and this small town off the highway was the last sort of place he ever thought he'd be spending a Saturday morning in spring.

It had been an early morning, of course, and an anxious night before it, with that call to the tip line coming in just as he was leaving for cocktails with the Rockefellers.

He yawned again, then took a sip from his silver-plated coffee carafe, pulling his hand-stitched jacket a little closer and adjusting his cashmere scarf under his chin.

Tired or not, anxious night or not, today was going to be wonderful. He was going to be reunited with the star of his poodle empire, and things would return to normal. No—they would be even better than normal. There was nothing like a little tragedy to help build a brand like his. Once they witnessed the love of a lost pet reunited with its owner, everyone in America was going to want a Poodles, Inc., poodle for their very own.

He pursed his lips, considering. It might have been slightly better if the separation had lasted a few days more. He could have made good use of a full week of frantic searching, with all those nationwide headlines and television interviews. As it was, things were ending a shade abruptly. But that couldn't be helped now. At least the child who'd phoned in the tip had called late, forcing the reunion to wait until the morning. That had given him time to alert the media, ensuring they'd be there to capture the moment properly.

He looked over his shoulder at the cars following behind his limo. Reporters, photographers, even a television crew with their newfangled camera truck. And every last one a friend he could trust to give his historic, tear-filled reunion with Masterpiece the coverage it deserved.

Finally, the view through the windows began to show a proper town, the houses getting closer together, then a car lot, a cinema, a bank. The limo sailed along, drawing an enormous amount of attention. It was still early, of course, but Count Pulaski saw enough people out to satisfy him. It would be good to have a crowd of gawking locals providing background to the newspaper photographs.

He resisted the urge to wave benevolently as his limo passed a group of mothers pushing strollers. This town would be talking about his visit for decades to come. These people would see history in the making. They didn't know how lucky they were.

"We're coming up to it, sir," Charles the chauffeur called, in that velvet-smooth English accent Count Pulaski had always secretly resented.

He nodded to his driver and went back to gazing out the window, beginning his mental preparation to cry at the sight of the dog. His right hand went to the seat beside him, absently patting the satin pillow from the front window of Poodles, Inc. It would be a comfort to Masterpiece after his long ordeal being stuck in this nowhere town. The poor thing must be absolutely desperate to get back to New York! Much more importantly, the pillow would show the world what a caring, thoughtful dog owner Count Pulaski was.

The car slowed, making a wide, looping arc against the traffic as Charlie pulled it to the curb. The engine quieted. Count Pulaski looked out.

They were in a dingy sort of downtown, a string of

forgettable businesses lining both sides of the street. And there, just ahead, tacked on at the very end, was the appointed meeting place: Dayton Family Shoeshine.

Count Pulaski took a deep breath and let it out slowly, readying the flood of emotions he hoped to unleash for the cameras and giving the media caravan behind him time to catch up and unload.

The media began setting up on the sidewalk, reporters in trench coats and trilby hats elbowing for position, flipping open their pads to take notes on the weather, the shoeshine, the overall scene. None of them seemed at all impressed by the meeting place, but he hoped the honest, small-town, working-class modesty of the location would add a wonderful edge to the story.

He checked his diamond-studded watch. Nine on the dot. But the shoeshine shop was still dark, its sign indicating it was closed. Where was the girl, then? Where was his dog?

The gathering locals were becoming a real crowd. Even the people eating breakfast at the waffle house across the street had left their tables to stand at the window, peering out with their hands full of toast and thick mugs of coffee.

At last, something happened. The blind inside the door of the shoeshine swung slightly, and a moment later the door cracked open. A girl appeared, clearly struggling to keep something inside with her foot as she squeezed through.

Excellent, thought Count Pulaski. *That must be Masterpiece, desperate to be reunited.*

The girl finally tugged the door shut behind her and turned to face the crowd. Cameras flashed, reporters shouted questions, and the gawking locals began chattering. The girl made an effort to hold her head high, but from her expression, Count Pulaski thought she looked like she was about to be sick.

He rolled his eyes. Had the girl not been expecting so much attention? Did she not understand how big a celebrity he was? Small-town children really did know nothing.

He examined her critically. She was a plain girl, mousy brown hair, unremarkable pale skin, a suggestion of freckles. And what on earth was she wearing? That dress did not fit, for one thing—and, really, puffy sleeves? Velvet bows? Did she think this meeting was a child's birthday party? Or a Sunday school concert?

He sighed in frustration. This was *not* the photogenic child with a perfect smile he'd been hoping for. One more irritation.

Still, the girl's wide eyes had found the limousine. She stood alone on the sidewalk, staring.

His moment had arrived.

Count Pulaski yawned one last time, fluffed his cashmere scarf, and gave the signal to Charles.

The chauffeur got out. Count Pulaski's door was opened with a bow. And amid a barrage of shouts and cheers and flashing cameras, the poodle king of Manhattan went to meet the shoeshine girl of Banbridge.

Twenty-Three
A HANDSHAKE

The count was tall—that was the first thing Joanie noticed. Tall and imposing in that stylish black coat and silky cashmere scarf and those shiny, shiny shoes. He was a real celebrity, a star from that other place, the world on her walls. And he was walking toward her. Right now.

Count Pulaski approached slowly, keeping his eyes on hers. He was probably doing it to be polite, but Joanie found it a little threatening, so she looked past him at the limousine instead. She'd never seen one in real life. Or a chauffeur. The chauffeur was shorter than the count, but very handsome. He was also the only person not watching them. He was gazing at something across the street, smiling like he knew a joke no one else did. Joanie glanced over but couldn't see anything over the heads of the watching crowd.

Then the count was standing before her, and she pulled her eyes back to him. The crowd hushed.

"Hello," the man said into the sudden stillness. "I'm Count Alexi Pulaski."

Joanie stared. The count had the most perfect Russian accent. His rings glittered in the sun. His spicy, flowery cologne was making her dizzy.

"It—it's very nice to meet you," she said. She thrust out a hand. "I'm Joanie Dayton."

Count Pulaski blinked down at her hand, then held out his own. They shook. Someone gave a cheer, and the crowd broke into applause.

Count Pulaski visibly relaxed, his face breaking into a beaming smile, and began waving his free hand for the flashing cameras.

As for Joanie, she felt flat-out confused. Why were they doing this in front of a crowd? And why was the crowd applauding? What was Count Pulaski doing things so slowly for, like he was acting out a part in a play? Why hadn't he immediately asked to see Lucky? If it was Joanie arriving somewhere to get her dog back, she would have been jumping up and down with impatience.

She closed her sharp right eye, examining the count with her soft one. He looked foggy and dreamlike, his mustache and neat hair setting off his handsome, warm face. His watch sparkled. His rings glowed. His scarf floated like a cloud. He looked exactly as a Russian count who ran a poodle empire in New York should.

Then she switched, and immediately felt a shiver scurry down her back. It was like looking at an entirely different person. Through her sharp eye, Count Pulaski's smile looked fixed, like it was held up with wire, and his teeth were long and coffee-stained. His heavy jewelry looked thick and uncomfortable. And there was something behind his eyes that made her want to frown.

So, which was the real Count Pulaski? One version looked like the pictures she'd seen in the papers: a star, glowing with glamour and influence and style. The other looked like a normal man, just anybody, working hard at pretending to be something he wasn't. Seen through her sharp eye, up close, Joanie didn't think she liked Count Pulaski very much.

All at once she realized the applause had stopped, though the handshake was still happening. It had been going for quite some time, and Count Pulaski was gazing down at Joanie with a look of barely contained alarm.

She opened both eyes wide, trying to look normal, and gave him her best smile.

Count Pulaski smiled back, looking hugely relieved, then with absolutely no warning at all sank to his knees, clasping his hands in front of her.

"Please," he said, in a dramatic, carrying voice. The reporters' pencils flew over their notebooks, taking down every word. "When I heard someone had called the hotline, I hardly dared believe it could be true. Tell me, Joanie Dayton: Was it you who found and cared for my beloved friend? My Masterpiece?"

Joanie blinked at him. Of course it was her. He knew that. They had spoken on the phone. This man was seeming less and less authentic by the minute.

A tiny seed of doubt opened inside her. Was this even Count Pulaski? What if the number in the paper was a hoax, and this was an imposter? What if she was sending her best friend into the arms of another dognapper?

And even if this *was* Pulaski, how happy could Lucky be going back to him? The count could provide a life of luxury, sure, but what about friendship? Could Lucky really be happy with this man?

Was it too late to change her mind? Too late to take it back?

Count Pulaski and the crowd were waiting for a reply.

"Yes," said Joanie. "It was me. I found him." Her mind was spinning, and she felt a sudden need to explain. "But I didn't steal him! I don't know how he got all the way out here! He was stuck under a crate in the alley, and I rescued him and gave him a bath and took care of him because he was dirty and hungry! And I gave him a good home and loved him even though now he has to go back . . ."

Joanie trailed off, heat growing on her face.

Count Pulaski didn't blink as he stared down at her. Then he laughed.

"Child, child!" he said. "No one ever for one moment thought *you* were the dognapper!" His voice was soothing, but Joanie caught an edge of irritation beneath it. Like she was saying the wrong things, ruining the moment somehow.

"But now," the count continued, "I think you and I have done enough talking, don't you?" He got back to his feet, giving his coat a little flourish. "Now, where is my beloved pride and joy? Where is Masterpiece?"

Joanie gulped. "He's—he's inside." It was all happening too fast. "I'll get him."

She could feel the muscles of her heart tearing one by one as she turned her back on the count, the newspaper crews, the television cameras, the watching crowds, and walked up the steps of Dayton Family Shoeshine.

She reached the door handle. She turned. She pushed.

Then she gasped, her hands flying to her mouth as the door swung open.

There were footsteps, and someone hurried up behind her.

"What is it?" said Count Pulaski. "What is wrong?"

Then he gasped, too. They stood in the doorway together, speechless at the sight of the shop.

The store was a disaster. All Joanie's cleaning had been undone. Shoelaces were tangled across the floor; papers, shoeboxes, eyelets, and polish tins lay scattered everywhere. And there was no sign of Lucky.

The slam of a car door made Joanie jump, and she turned on instinct, looking out over the crowd just in time to see the powder-blue sedan across the street roar into life, a woman in a scarf and sunglasses behind the wheel. A heartbeat later the car was disappearing down Main Street, a familiar little face barking and barking behind the shining rear window all the way.

Twenty-Four
A CHASE

Masterpiece had been utterly shocked to be left alone inside Dayton Family Shoeshine.

First Joanie had delivered the devastating news that she was handing him back to Count Pulaski, then she'd stepped outside—blocking him in with her foot!—and shut the door in his face, leaving him trapped with his own desperate thoughts: Was Count Pulaski already here? When had Joanie gotten in touch with him? Most of all, why hadn't she understood that Masterpiece wanted to stay? He didn't *want* to go back to Count Pulaski. And Joanie didn't want him to either, from what she'd said, but it sounded like she had to. All because of money.

Masterpiece had never given much thought to money. Humans did seem to fuss over it, but since they had made it up in the first place, that made sense. It was like a toy they all wanted to play with. Only some of them had plenty of time with the toy and others not enough, and for some reason it made a big difference in how they lived. It was all very odd.

But now Joanie had said that because of it, she was having to return him to Count Pulaski for a reward that would help her family be okay.

Well, Masterpiece definitely wanted to help the Daytons be okay—he just didn't want to have to leave them to do it. He decided right then and there that he would come up with some other way for Joanie to make money. For right now, though, he was trapped inside the shoeshine shop, alone.

He could hear a growing noise from outside, along with the flashing of camera bulbs. Masterpiece was used to those, but he knew Joanie wouldn't be. He wished he could see what was happening to her. All of the blinds were down, but he managed to get his paws on the windowsill and peer through a gap.

There was a crowd out there, a big one, all watching Joanie as she . . . shook hands with Count Pulaski.

Masterpiece trembled. He hadn't seen the count in two whole days. Somehow that already felt like a lifetime ago.

Joanie and Count Pulaski began talking. It was so strange looking at them together, like seeing the subjects from two separate museum paintings having a chat. It made him feel dizzy.

Between the flash of one camera and the next, Masterpiece was hit with an idea. He would need to get to Joanie's house to make it happen, but it might work. It should work. It *had* to work!

He would have to face Count Pulaski to do it, though. That could be tricky. Hopefully, the count wouldn't recognize him. Humans relied so much on sight, and he did have his new haircut, and his splotches and stains from the alley. It was like a disguise! People in this town had certainly thought he looked disreputable. Maybe Count Pulaski would, too. Maybe he could convince him.

That just left the biggest obstacle: escaping the shop. He darted around, looking for a way out, but both doors were shut tight and the windows were closed.

Well, he would just have to try and slip past Joanie whenever she came back in. It would be tricky, but it was looking like his only option.

A thud suddenly sounded from the back of the shop, then a cracking noise. Masterpiece turned, his ears up. What was *that*? He ran into the back room.

The cracking sound came again, then a clang, then a rush of air as the back door swung open and a woman carrying a crowbar and a gigantic purse stepped into Dayton Family Shoeshine.

Masterpiece could have howled.

Her coat was blue today instead of red, and she wore huge sunglasses and a scarf wrapped around her face. But he would have known that dry flowery smell and those tight brown curls anywhere. It was the woman he had gotten away from once already. It was the dognapper.

"Holy moly, what happened to you?!" the woman shouted. She shut the ruined door behind her, blocking his chance to escape. "Why'd that girl shave and paint you up like that? You look like a palomino horse from a backwater circus!"

Masterpiece had never once in his life shown his teeth and growled, but he did so now.

"Hey, hey, none of that." The lady shook her head. "You may look like a menace, but we both know you're the best-behaved little show dog in the world. Besides, I'm your friend, remember? I'm taking you to a nice place by the shore. And soon *I'll* be the one handing you over to that complete charlatan smiling for the cameras out front. Honestly, you should be thanking me! If I were you, I wouldn't want Pulaski seeing me looking like I belonged in this crappy town. He might decide to leave you here forever!"

She laughed and took a step forward. Masterpiece stepped back.

"Oh, don't be like that," the woman said. "You know I've got you cornered, so you may as well come along quietly. I can promise for sure I won't be losing you again!"

She strode forward, making a sudden grab for him, and Masterpiece turned and ran.

He ran under the front counter. The woman followed. He darted out, sending papers and shoeboxes flying, and made a dash to the shoeshine chairs. The woman cut him off. He backed into a display of laces, knocking them from their rack, and the woman pounced, triumph in her eyes. At the last second, Masterpiece slipped free, jumping right up onto the work counter, batting shoe polish tins left and right.

The chase continued, round and round the room, Masterpiece bracing every second for the front door to open. What would Joanie do when she came in to this? Or Count Pulaski? He was just opening his mouth to bark for attention when the dognapper finally nabbed him.

"Gotcha!" the lady cried, her long-nailed fingers wrapping around him as he slipped between her high-heeled shoes. She lifted him up, squeezing him in one hand and opening her giant purse with the other. Before he could think, Masterpiece had been dumped inside, and the catch closed with a click.

The purse was lined with satin and smelled like leather, peppermint breath drops, and, ugh, cat hair. He flailed, turning over and over in the darkness. The woman gave the purse a shake.

"Stop that!" she said. "Stop it this instant! You've been caught, and we are getting back on the road, and that's all there is to it!"

The bag bounced as the woman hurried out the rear of the shop. Masterpiece could hear the muffled sounds of outside, the woman's heels on concrete, the babble of the reporters in the crowd.

He barked, desperately. He couldn't leave Joanie now! Not like this!

He kept barking, over and over, but the woman hacked her own loud, fake coughs, drowning him out. She was moving fast, so she must have been skirting the very edge of the crowd anyway, but Masterpiece kept trying. He could not give up.

Then there was the thunk of a car door opening, and he was set down. The door slammed, and Masterpiece kicked and squirmed for all he was worth, finally tearing the giant purse open. He popped out, breathing hard as he got his bearings, and his blood ran cold.

It was happening again.

He was back in the powder-blue sedan.

He stared wildly out at the crowd, hoping someone would see. But they all had their backs to him, watching the excitement outside Dayton Family Shoeshine. No one had noticed the real event happening behind them.

He threw himself at the window, barking, just as the woman brought the engine roaring to life, and for one single shining moment his eyes found Joanie, his own sweet sunshine girl, staring over the crowd at him from the front steps of the shop. Then the dognapper squealed her tires, pulled onto Main Street, and took off, speeding for the highway as fast as her car could go.

Twenty-Five
A SPEED BUMP

Holly Knickerbocker was having a marvelous day.

She had eaten her triumphant maple-syrup breakfast at that awful hotel, packed up, checked out, and gotten a good parking spot across from the dumpy shoeshine. And then she had gotten what she'd wanted.

She reached over to stroke Katerina, who had slept the whole exciting morning away on the passenger seat, only waking once the dog arrived and began making that terrible racket.

Katerina stretched her legs, rubbed her cheek briefly against Holly's wrist, then tucked her head under her paws and went back to sleep. She was warm and comfortable, and grateful they finally had the silly dog and all this deeply boring bother could be over.

"You know, you didn't have to make me chase you down

like that," Holly called to the back seat. Masterpiece was still barking—at her, at the car, at the world passing by. He seemed genuinely upset about being rescued. "My plan went perfectly, apart from you making all that mess. Now we just have to find our way out of this nowhere town."

She scanned the street signs and turned right onto Maple.

"That girl sure has caused me some trouble, though," Holly went on. "Why on earth did she ruin your pretty coat like that? Was she trying to hide you? Like a disguise?"

The dog's protests began to falter, becoming more forlorn as house after house flew by.

Holly snorted. "Well, it didn't fool me one second. Though it would probably work on Pulaski, huh? That man's oblivious to anything not pressed and polished and tied up in gold. Speaking of tied up—hey, listen!" She glared into the rearview mirror. The poodle met her eyes, then looked away. "There will be no more running off, do you hear me? I'm not stopping this car until we get to my beach house, where you will stay in a nice secure crate in a nice secure basement until your hair grows back and you look the way you ought to. Got it?"

A sudden jolt shook the car, and all three passengers bounced into the air.

"What the—?!" Holly slammed on the brakes, bringing the sedan to a skidding halt.

Panting, she pushed up the scarf that had slid over her eyes and surveyed the damage. Mercifully, the car seemed fine. Masterpiece was on his back, untangling himself from the handles and contents of her giant purse. Katerina had suffered the worst of it, bouncing tail over whiskers right off her seat and onto the floor mat. She let out a hissing growl as she climbed back up, murder in her eyes, and began smoothing her ruffled fur.

"Whoo!" said Holly, laughing. "Everybody okay? Looks like we hit one of those newfangled speed bumps. Wacky place to put one, though, out in a neighborhood. What's it supposed to be protecting?"

A red rubber ball banged off the windshield.

Holly's head whipped around.

A crowd of children, all elementary school age by the look of them, were blocking the street ahead.

Holly wound down her window. "Hey!" she shouted. "Watch where you're throwing those balls, kids! And move, why don't you? I've got places to be!"

She gave a double honk on the horn, expecting the children to let her through. But instead the group exchanged glances, closed ranks, and began walking toward her.

They were clean, well-dressed children, obviously from families with money, but something about the way they sauntered made the back of Holly's neck prickle.

The children spread out as they approached, surrounding the car. A tall girl and a boy with slicked-back blond hair positioned themselves beside Holly's open window, crossing their arms in unison.

"Well, well, well. What do you think you're doin', lady?" said the girl.

"Yeah," said the boy. "This here is *our* street. We're having ourselves a kickball tournament."

The girl nodded. "And you're ruining it."

Clearly, these were the ringleaders.

Holly was not in the mood to be messed with. Eyes blazing, she stuck her head out the window and let them have it as only a New Yorker could.

"Listen up, you overgrown pill bugs! You've got five seconds to scram before I put my foot down and drive this machine right over your sorry behinds!"

To her astonishment, the kids didn't scram. Instead, the girl and boy stepped in closer, leaning themselves nonchalantly against the powder-blue curves of her car.

"See, the thing is," said the boy, "you messed up our tournament, lady. Messed it up bad."

The tall girl tilted her head. "That's right. And the way we see it, that means you owe us some compensation. Financial compensation. Ain't that right, Jerry?"

"Oh, that's right, Margo."

Holly gaped at them. These horrible children were clearly imitating those radio detective dramas, or even gangster movies. What were their parents thinking, exposing impressionable youths to stories like that?

"Now listen here," she began, waving a threatening finger at the pair, "if you think for one minute—"

"Hey! Hey, look!"

The cry came from the back of the car, where more of the awful children were pressing their hands and faces to the glass.

"It's that dog! The mangy one!"

"Hey, yeah! Jokey's dog!"

All the children began shouting and pointing. Masterpiece jumped up, barking.

Katerina, deciding enough was absolutely enough, abandoned her seat and squeezed herself into the safety of the darkness beneath it, invisible except for the tip of her lashing tail.

"So, what you doing with that dog, lady?" the tall girl asked, pretending to check her nails. "We know that's not *your* dog."

"That's Jokey Dayton's dog," agreed the boy. "Why do *you* have Jokey Dayton's dog?"

Holly found herself gaping again. Behind her a boy exclaimed, "That's the dog that peed on my bike!" and the others all laughed and began telling him he smelled.

"You know what I think?" the tall girl said, gazing up the road like she didn't have a care in the world. "I think you shouldn't have that dog no more, lady."

"That's right," said the boy. "I think you'd better let us take him off your hands."

"What? No!" Holly spluttered. These children were nothing but criminals!

"I think that's a fine idea." The girl signaled to a short boy on the other side of Holly's car.

"Wait! Stop! How dare you?" Holly was trying to shout in too many directions at once. Before she could do a thing, the short boy had opened the passenger door, leaned in, and scooped little Masterpiece, the world's most valuable dog, into his arms.

"NO!" screamed Holly. She fumbled for her seat belt, her elbow banging the horn, but just as she got free, the two criminal ringleaders leaned hard against her door, shoving it closed.

"What are you doing?" Holly wailed. "Let. Me. Out!"

But the children didn't let her out. They braced

themselves against the door, laughing as she pushed and shoved from the inside.

The rest of the gang obviously liked the idea, because they launched the same attack on the other three doors.

Holly felt like the ground was collapsing under her.

"Listen!" she shouted, using every bit of her lung power. "That is *my* dog, who was stolen from *me*. Got it?! And if you don't give him back right this instant, I will have the law on you!"

The children laughed! They laughed and began rocking her precious car! From under the passenger seat, Katerina began to yowl.

The boy holding Masterpiece paraded his way to the front, waving the poodle triumphantly at the windshield. He had a good grip, but the dog was twisting and struggling like anything. Holly's stomach clenched. If Masterpiece got free again, all her scheming would be for nothing.

"Guess he's our dog now," the boy crowed. "We're gonna sell him back to Jokey! See how much she really loves him!"

The other children whooped in appreciation.

"That's right! Hold him hostage!"

"Yeah!"

"Careful, Michael," called the tall boy suddenly. "He might try and—"

"EW!" cried the boy holding Masterpiece.

"—pee again."

Sure enough, the little dog was peeing with great enthusiasm all over the horrible child. Holly chortled in glee for exactly two seconds, but then the boy dropped the dog, and her heart plummeted like a broken elevator. With a scrabbling of paws, Masterpiece tore down the street, across a well-kept lawn, around the next corner, and out of sight.

Holly heard her own scream echo in her ears.

"Geez, lady," said the tall girl. "Pipe down. It's just some stray mutt."

Holly was so angry she could barely speak. These terrible, awful, horrible children had just lost her the greatest scoop, grandest prize, and biggest headline ever!

Her mind raced. The animal was gone, disappeared into the suburban waste of small-town New Jersey. But he had to go *somewhere*. Maybe she could figure it out.

These kids had said the Dayton girl—what kind of name was Jokey?—loved him, maybe. Would the little rat try and get back to her? Maybe return to the shoeshine and skulk around until the crowd went home? It wasn't a great lead, but it was her only one. She had to get back there and start checking the neighboring alleys, behind the shop, everywhere!

Holly Knickerbocker locked eyes with the tall girl and put her car in reverse.

"I'm going to count to three," she said, "and then I'm going to hold down this horn and scream blue murder until every grown-up in a five-mile radius comes running. And I guarantee you will all be in big, *big* trouble then. One."

The children glared at her, but worry flickered across a few faces.

"Two."

The tall girl gulped. The slick-haired boy lifted one hand from the door. The other children exchanged glances.

"Three!" shouted Holly, and she punched the horn with her fist and held it there, blaring.

All the children jumped clear, and Holly seized her chance, gunning the sedan backward up Maple Street. She barely even noticed as she bounced over that absurd speed bump again, her head almost hitting the ceiling.

Katerina sure noticed, as she was flung across the floor like a bouncy ball. She lay in a heap under the glove box, every one of her claws stabbing into the mat, spitting curses for the dog that had made her perfect life so unbearable.

Behind the wheel, Holly jerked the car around, and, with a final rude hand gesture to the mob of horrible children, drove for all she was worth back to Dayton Family Shoeshine.

Twenty-Six
A CONFRONTATION

"We have to go after that car! She's got Lucky!"

Joanie was hardly aware she was shouting. Or that she was stepping out of the doorway, heading toward the crowd, her eyes fixed on the road where the powder-blue car had vanished.

A large, gold-ringed hand appeared, blocking her path.

"Now then," Count Pulaski said. "I think you should explain before you go running off, miss. Where is my dog you have promised me?"

"He was right here!" Tears welled behind Joanie's eyes. She tugged away from Count Pulaski and waved a hand at the chaos of the shop. "He was waiting inside while I went out to meet you. But it was clean in here before! That lady— she must have snuck in and taken him! I saw him in the back of her car! You have to believe me!"

Count Pulaski stepped inside, Joanie right behind him, and ran his eyes over the shop. He gave a sniff, the corners of his mouth turning down, and Joanie realized he was judging what he saw. He was looking down on her family's second home, the store her parents had built with years of hard work and sacrifice.

She had another flash of disorientation as the reality of the situation settled over her. Count Alexi Pulaski was actually standing in her family's shoe repair shop. For as long as she could remember, she'd dreamed of getting out of Banbridge, of growing up and seeing the world. Now the world had come to her. And it was not at all like she had imagined.

The curtain dividing the back room from the front rippled suddenly, and Joanie ran forward, her heart leaping. But when she reached it, she saw it had only been a breeze coming in through the back door, which was standing wide. The frame was cracked and splintered.

"Look! Look! See?" she said, pointing. "Someone broke in! They must have been waiting until the coast was clear!"

The dignified count eyed the door, the messy shop, and finally Joanie.

"It is possible, is it not, that you might be tricking me?" he said.

Joanie's face flushed with anger. Someone had just

dognapped Lucky! They were getting away! There was no time for this silly discussion! She opened her mouth, but the count held up a finger.

"No—I think you will be polite and hear me out. What is more likely? That you found my beloved Masterpiece *here*." He gestured around, his face clearly showing his feelings. "Or that you, a poor girl—a girl with big dreams, I think I can guess—decided to invent a story to try and get herself the substantial reward?"

"I wouldn't! I didn't! He really was here! I *did* find him!"

"Or perhaps it is not the reward you are after, but the attention?" Count Pulaski gave her a condescending, coffee-stained smile. "You come up with this scheme, and look! You have managed to get the famous, respected Count Alexi Pulaski to come see you. You have arrived early and prepared your family shop. You invent this story of a mysterious woman and a break-in and a blue getaway car." He put his fingers to his head, rubbing his temples. "In short, you put yourself into the story. You force your way into my very real tragedy and grab as much fame as you can. It was a bold plan, miss, I will give you that. If I were not so unspeakably upset, I would almost be impressed."

Joanie had heard of people being struck speechless before but had never experienced it for herself. She did now. Count Pulaski's iron certainty that this whole thing had been a trick was so incredibly wrong she didn't even know where to begin.

Outside, the chatter of the crowd was growing louder. They couldn't see inside the shop, and must have been wondering why the dog wasn't appearing, why Count Pulaski wasn't bringing the grateful little animal out into the sunlight so they could clap and cheer and photograph the reunited celebrity duo.

Inside, the count shook his head. "Well, I hope it was worth it," he said. "You will receive attention for this, Joanie Dayton, certainly. But I do not think it will be the kind you would wish."

Then he turned his back and walked out the door.

Joanie stood alone in the shop, hearing the excited roar of the crowd, the reporters shouting questions.

"What's the story, Count?"

"Where's the poodle?"

"Why aren't you showing us the dog?"

"Where's Masterpiece?"

Joanie did not want to go back outside. Lucky was gone. Stolen right in front of her. And now the count thought she had been trying to trick him, that she had never found his dog in the first place. Her heart felt as wrecked as the shop as she realized that she had not only lost her friend forever, she had lost her chance at the reward, the money that would save her family and make her parents smile again.

Everything had gone wrong.

She stood there, trying to decide whether to sneak out the back or just hide in the shop until her parents arrived. They would be on their way soon.

Count Pulaski stood on the sidewalk, framed by the open door while reporters crowded around, still shouting out questions. The count raised his hands.

"Friends, my friends," he called, his rich voice soaring over the crowd. "I am sorry to have to report that we have all been taken in. Masterpiece, my beloved dog and precious companion who was stolen from me, is not here."

Gasps filled the air, followed by more shouting. Joanie cringed as she heard the words *that girl's a fraud* and *the little liar* coming from more than one voice. She peeked through a gap in the blinds to see.

The crowd was bigger than ever, and Joanie recognized some familiar faces gathered behind the wall of reporters: Harold Apple from the garage; Cathy Muffler, who owned the diner; Earl Greene from the store with all the televisions. Was anyone working today? It seemed like the whole town had come out to see the excitement.

Count Pulaski was waving a hand, trying to regain control.

"Why would the girl lie, Count?" shouted one of the reporters. "Was she trying to get the reward?"

"I cannot say for certain what this poor child was after," answered Pulaski. He sounded warm, concerned, and so very reasonable. "It may have been an attempt to get money, or it may have been a plea for attention. You will notice she is keeping out of the spotlight now she has been caught, however. The one thing I know for certain is she does not have a dog."

"Oh, she's got a dog, all right!" shouted a voice.

Joanie peered around the crowd and felt her stomach clench. Daniel Payton-Price was pushing his way to the front, Mayor Archer and his wife, Eileen, behind him.

"Daniel Payton-Price," the businessman said, striding forward to seize Count Pulaski's hand. "Upstanding citizen. And Payton-Price is hyphenated," he added, winking at the reporters. He turned to face the crowd. "The Dayton girl does have a dog," he called. "But it's no show dog. It's the meanest, worst-behaved, mangiest mutt you've ever seen. It's been terrorizing the whole town since it showed up!"

"That's right!" yelled Harold Apple.

"It tore up my diner!" called Cathy Muffler.

"And paraded around my hotel!" shouted an elderly lady in dramatic makeup Joanie didn't know.

"It's been a menace!" hollered the mayor, before seizing

Count Pulaski's hand. "Calvin B. Archer," he said, pumping vigorously. "Mayor of Banbridge. And this is my wife, Eileen." The couple squeezed in on one side of the count, trapping him between them and Daniel Payton-Price.

"The whole Dayton family is trouble," Daniel Payton-Price said. "I bet you anything they found a stray and thought they could pass it off as your poodle for the reward!"

"Say," said Eileen Archer, eyeing the gaggle of reporters from her new vantage point. "Where's Holly? I mean, Miss Knickerbocker? Shouldn't she be front and center on a story like this?"

"Holly Knickerbocker?" Count Pulaski looked surprised. "The society columnist?"

"Yes!" Mayor Archer puffed up his chest. "She's here in Banbridge, doing a piece on our town! I'm sure she wouldn't want to miss out on this piece of history in action!"

"Has anybody seen Holly Knickerbocker?" shouted Eileen Archer.

The crowd looked around, murmuring. Joanie was sure most of the locals had no idea who Holly Knickerbocker was, but they seemed to be enjoying the thrill of celebrity nonetheless. Joanie was just happy the barrage of complaints against her family had been stopped by the distraction.

Shouting broke out way at the back of the crowd, and all the heads turned.

"Look!" someone cried. "There she is! It's her!"

Joanie pressed her face right up to the blinds, too curious to be careful, and saw a woman being nudged forward. The woman seemed incredibly reluctant to be the center of attention, but that wasn't what made Joanie's mouth drop open.

Joanie recognized that expensive silk headscarf.

She recognized those sunglasses.

This was the dognapper from the powder-blue sedan!

"Come on, Miss Knickerbocker!" Mayor Archer called. "Come right up to the front here! A celebrity reporter like yourself deserves an exclusive!"

The other reporters didn't seem to like the sound of that, and from what was visible of her face, neither did Holly Knickerbocker. Still, the crowd parted, closing behind her as she went, leaving her with no choice but to join the group in front of the shop.

Anger rose in Joanie at the sight of her, and the memory of her dear, darling, wonderful Lucky barking in the back seat of her car. This woman had broken into her family shop and stolen her best friend. And now she was back. For what? For the reward? Was she going to hand Lucky over to Count Pulaski now that Joanie had been disgraced and taken out of the picture? That would be the most unfair thing in the world!

Joanie's anger bubbled over, and before she could think twice, she charged out of the shop, ignoring the shouts and sudden camera flashes, and marched right into Holly Knickerbocker's path.

Holly pulled up short. "Oh, it's you," she snapped, her high, harsh voice bouncing off the shop and ringing over the scene. "What do you think you're doing, child? And what are you *wearing*?" She gave Joanie's best dress a slow look up and down. "Have we traveled back in time to 1946?"

The crowd laughed. The reporters took pictures.

"Where is my dog?" Joanie said, drawing herself up. There were so many people around her, so many strangers, so many eyes watching. But these rich, fancy, famous people had come into *her* town, insulted her, wrecked her shop, and called her a liar in front of everyone. She was not going to back down.

"I know you took him!" she shouted at Holly Knicker-bocker. "I saw you drive off with him in your car!"

"What an imagination you have, girl," Holly Knickerbocker said, adjusting her scarf. "I have no idea what you're taking about. Though from what I've heard, you do seem to have trouble with the truth." She looked up at Count Pulaski. "Hello, Alexi. It's been far too long. What a world this is, when young children in America abuse the trust of their elders and the faith of the hardworking reporters who bring us the truth."

The crowd chattered in agreement, and Holly stepped forward, forcing Joanie back.

"I'm not lying!" Joanie shouted, but she could feel the mood moving against her. Count Pulaski was holding out a hand to Holly, also looking sorrowful, and people around her were shaking their heads and muttering about "kids today." One old man even shook a finger at Joanie and tsked.

She stumbled back until she was standing alone on a clear patch of sidewalk.

What on earth could she do? The woman in the scarf was lying, but how could she prove it? And where was the blue car? Where had the woman taken Lucky?

Count Pulaski and Holly Knickerbocker exchanged air kisses, then looped arms. They looked even more fancy and famous standing side by side, especially with the Archers on one side and Daniel Payton-Price all slicked back and shiny on the other. Daniel waved to a group of friends in the crowd, and the mayor and Eileen Archer began telling the reporters near them how they had taken Holly to lunch to help with her research, and how they were now very close friends.

Joanie was beginning to consider simply running away when a fresh wave of excitement started at the other side of the crowd. People were pulling apart, letting a group through, but Joanie couldn't make out who they were until the last line of grown-ups parted. Then she groaned.

It was the mean kids. The Archers, the Payton-Prices, and their awful attendants. Joanie felt the ground spin beneath her. The most horrible moment of her life had somehow gotten worse. Why couldn't they just leave her alone for one day?

And why did they all look like they'd been running?

"Jerry? Michael?" said Mayor Archer, looking surprised. "What are you doing here?"

"Same to you, Margo," said Daniel Payton-Price. "I thought you kids were organizing a dodgeball tournament this morning."

"Kickball," said Margo. "And we were, but then something more interesting happened."

Joanie braced herself, ready for whatever horrible thing these children were going to say about her. But to her surprise, Jerry Archer planted his feet, smoothed back his slick blond hair, and pointed directly at Holly Knickerbocker.

Holly's smile had vanished. She tried to get free from Count Pulaski, tugging at her arm, but before she could, Jerry spoke.

"We," he said, his voice echoing over the hushed crowd, "want answers."

"Answers?" asked the mayor.

"Answers to what?" asked Daniel Payton-Price.

"This lady drove her car into our kickball game," said Jerry. "I looked up from scoring a run and this big blue car was heading right for us. So, of course, I chucked the ball to warn her. And then she was rude to us! So rude you would not believe it!"

Holly Knickerbocker bristled.

"*I* was rude? It was you little brats who—"

"And it gets worse!" Impressively, Margo Payton-Price was able to speak over her. "She also had a dog in the back! A stolen dog! And we know who's it was. It was Jokey—I mean, Joanie Dayton's little runt!"

For one moment there was total silence over Main Street. Joanie thought she heard the faint singing of a robin in the distance.

Then the shouting began.

"LIES! LIES! DEFAMATION BEFORE WITNESSES!" bellowed Holly Knickerbocker.

"You did! We saw it!" yelled the children.

"I did, too!" chimed in Joanie. She never imagined she would be on the same side as these kids. "I saw you drive off with him! He's my dog! Give him back!"

"So there *was* a dog after all?" said Count Pulaski. He looked utterly bewildered. "But it wasn't my Masterpiece, was it? Why would you steal a local stray, Holly?"

"I STOLE NO DOGS! I CAME TO REPORT ON SOMEONE FINDING YOURS, BUT THIS LYING GIRL TRICKED US!"

"Hang on! You said you were here to do a piece on our town!" said Mayor Archer. "Was that a lie, too?"

"And you've been here for days," put in Eileen Archer. "How could you have known this is where someone would pretend to find Count Pulaski's pet?"

"It *was* Joanie Dayton's dog!" Michael Archer shouted while the grown-ups argued. "It peed on me, just like it peed on my bike!" He tugged at his wet shirt. "See?"

The reporters backed away, but they snapped pictures, their pencils flying over their notebooks.

"IT'S ME WHO SHOULD BE ANGRY!" Holly Knicker-bocker screamed as Count Pulaski, the Archers, and the Payton-Prices surrounded her, all demanding explanations. "THOSE DARN KIDS COST ME THE DOG AGAIN, AND I WORKED TOO HARD—"

She cut off, but the damage was done.

Now everyone was rounding on Holly, demanding the truth, asking what she was really in town for, if the dog was really Masterpiece or not. Locals were squeezing in as close as they could get, standing on tiptoe to watch.

It was turning into the most exciting Saturday morning the town of Banbridge had ever known. And the excitement just kept coming as a small, spotted dog suddenly appeared, racing around legs, darting between the crowd and the shoeshine, and finally skidding to a halt to drop a mouthful of cardboard on the sidewalk at Joanie Dayton's feet.

Twenty-Seven
A STORM

To Masterpiece, joining the scene outside Dayton Family Shoeshine felt like running onstage in the middle of a play. He had attended many plays over the years with Count Pulaski, and this combination of arguing main characters and gawking locals reminded him of the final climactic scene in William Shakespeare's *Hamlet*. That scene had ended with most of the actors falling down, though, so he hoped this would turn out differently.

He was panting hard around his mouthful of cardboard, but he was happy. He had escaped from the dognapper, thanks to those awful children. He had put his plan in motion. Now he was back, and there was his Joanie!

He darted through the shoes and legs and dresses and pants, ignoring the shouts that followed him, and deposited the cardboard at his wonderful girl's feet.

In three heartbeats, Joanie's arms were around him, lifting him up, her face buried in his fur.

"Lucky, Lucky, Lucky, Lucky!" she said, over and over. She was squeezing hard, and it was wonderful. He had been so scared, meeting her eyes from the back of that car as it drove away with him trapped inside. What were the chances he could ever find her again? But he had. He had come back. Joanie *had* to understand now that he wanted to stay. That he wanted her to be his girl forever.

Being up in Joanie's arms gave Masterpiece a good view of what was happening. Count Pulaski had put himself in the center of everything, as usual. He was staring at Masterpiece, his eyes huge and his mouth hanging open. And he was arm in arm with the dognapper! She was staring at Masterpiece, too, and seemed to be trying to get her arm free, her face turning bright red.

Flanking them were the two rich men who had yelled and shouted inside the shoeshine the night before: Mayor Archer and Daniel Payton-Price. And standing alongside *them* were the awful children. Masterpiece wasn't sure how to feel about them anymore. They still seemed horrible, but they *had* saved him from the dognapper, after all.

And then there was Joanie, his Joanie, holding him tight and staring down every single one of them. He felt her heart thumping hard and fast.

"Where—where did that dog come from?!" cried Count Pulaski. The excited crowd quieted to listen.

"That's Jokey's dog!" answered the tall, mean girl. "The one that lady"—she pointed at the dognapper—"was trying to steal!"

"Why would anyone want to steal *that*?" sniffed a blond woman beside Mayor Archer. "It's a rude, ugly creature, and, from what I hear, totally out of control."

"Yes!" agreed the mayor. "It's been terrorizing the town. Am I right?" He turned to the crowd, which shouted and nodded in agreement.

Masterpiece frowned as he recognized many of the humans he'd encountered the day before. They thought *he* was causing problems? All he'd done was try and enjoy their businesses like anyone else. They were the ones failing to provide basic hospitality.

"That's definitely the troublemaker," said Daniel Payton-Price. He turned. "Tell me you didn't actually try to steal it, Miss Knickerbocker. I don't want to believe my own daughter is lying, but I really can't imagine why you'd want the thing."

The dognapper opened her mouth, then shut it again.

"She did try to steal it," the tall girl said firmly. "Scout's honor."

All the other kids nodded.

Something in the dognapper's face seemed to give way. "It—it climbed into my car on its own!" she shrieked. "I was the victim here. That mutt climbed in after me and tried to attack! I was driving it out of town, away from innocent civilians!"

"Liar!" That was Joanie. She stood up straight and tall as every face turned to her. "Lucky was safe in my family's shop. *You* broke in and took him!"

The watching crowd gave an "Ooo!" and swiveled their heads back to the dognapper.

"That's simply not . . ." the woman protested, but she didn't seem to know how to finish the sentence.

"Hold on one moment, please!" boomed Count Pulaski. He had hardly taken his eyes off Masterpiece. "Am I understanding correctly that this"—he took a step toward Joanie—"is the animal you called the hotline about, Miss Dayton? When we spoke, you told me you had found a dog you believed to be my missing Masterpiece. This is what brought me here today. And is this the dog you meant? You truly believe this is the most valuable dog in the world?"

"He *is* the most valuable dog in the world, no matter what!" answered Joanie, her arms squeezing even tighter. "And—" she faltered. "And I know he looks different, but I think—I'm certain . . . this really is Masterpiece."

The media began lobbing questions, all wanting to know if the count recognized him, if this was the missing dog, and Masterpiece shivered. This was it.

Count Pulaski took another step closer, staring down at him without blinking.

"I—I can't say. Not for certain. This animal is of course a poodle, but the hair is different, and the coloring is peculiar. That could be a disguise, as strange as that would be . . ." He gave Joanie a little bow. "Would you set the animal down, please? I need a clear view to make my assessment."

The media pressed forward, jockeying for camera angles, as Joanie carefully lowered Masterpiece to the pavement. He stood alone, every eye on all of Main Street watching.

With great formality, Count Pulaski knelt down beside him. Masterpiece had no choice but to look up.

It was so strange. This man had defined every moment of his life up to the day he was dognapped. This man had trained him in every trick, set every rule, made every decision. This man had given him friendship, but he had also treated Masterpiece like a performing toy. And Masterpiece understood now, by sheer force of contrast, how limited his life had been because of that.

Count Pulaski had never hugged Masterpiece the way Joanie did, or encouraged him to explore and be free, or shared his thoughts on long walks looking at flowers. He had valued Masterpiece, that was clear, but he had never told Masterpiece he was the best thing that had ever happened to him. He had never wept for joy to see him.

Count Pulaski was everything good from his old life, and everything missing from it, too.

Masterpiece turned his head to look up at Joanie. She had tears running down her cheeks. She smelled like so much sadness. She must have really believed she was letting him go, that Count Pulaski was about to sweep him up and take him away from her forever.

But that could not happen. He was determined. Joanie was his new life. It was his decision.

"Masterpiece?" said Count Pulaski softly. "Is that you?"

Masterpiece gave the count a wary glance and took a step back.

"Easy, easy," said the count. "All right, let's try something simple." He held out a hand, palm down. "Sit!"

It was difficult, after six whole years of habit and training, but Masterpiece did not sit. He remained standing. Count Pulaski frowned.

"Hmm. All right, lie down!"

Masterpiece sat and scratched his ear.

"Roll over!"

Masterpiece stood back up.

"It looks so much like him," Count Pulaski murmured. "So much. But . . ." He held a hand over Masterpiece's head, the fingers pinched like he was dangling a treat. "Dance! Come on, dance!"

Masterpiece growled.

The count snatched his hand back.

Masterpiece felt positively giddy. He had never growled at Count Pulaski before. Not once. And he had certainly never growled in front of so many people. It felt terrifying, and amazing. Growling was something bad dogs did, like barking. And speaking of barking . . .

He took a step toward Count Pulaski and gave his very loudest bark. He didn't woof, he didn't use the hollow-O sound or the polite indoor accent, he *barked*, with all his teeth and both his lungs.

Count Pulaski climbed to his feet as fast as his expensive pants would let him.

Masterpiece felt tremendous. First, he had refused the commands, now this! He kept on barking, at the count, at the mean rich men, at the dognapper and the awful children. He barked in celebration and excitement, in the joy of finally being free, running back and forth on the sidewalk, unable to keep his energy in.

"Look out!" the tall girl called. "That dog pees on people!"

Everyone backed away. The cluster of fancy grown-ups looked ridiculous now, pressed against the wall of Dayton Family Shoeshine. Masterpiece barked and barked, laughing.

"I've seen enough!" shouted Count Pulaski. "That dog is *not* my Masterpiece! No poodle of mine would ever be so ill-behaved, rude, or wild!"

Masterpiece gave one last happy howl and turned to his beloved Joanie. He ran for her, and she caught him up in her arms. It was the sweetest moment of his life. At last, she understood that he had made his choice. He had turned his back on Count Alexi Pulaski and everything that came with him, and he had chosen Joanie Dayton.

Count Pulaski's announcement was causing pandemonium among the media and watching crowd.

"So, this was a trick, then?!"

"Miss Knickerbocker, what was your part in all this? What do you say to the accusations of being a dognapper?"

"I told you that dog was trouble! I told you!"

"Count Pulaski, do you believe this was an attempt to defraud you of the reward money?"

"What does this mean for the search for Masterpiece?"

"Sir, do you intend to press charges against Joanie Dayton or her family?"

"What are we supposed to write about now?"

As the chaos grew, a few of the reporters finally remembered Joanie, who was pressing her face into Masterpiece's fur, her tears turned to happy ones.

"Miss Dayton, what made you believe this was the famous missing dog?"

"How do you respond to allegations this was all an elaborate hoax? Do you claim it was an honest mistake?"

"I can tell you that," said Margo Archer, pushing her way over with Jerry Payton-Price at her side. "Jokey here can't see right, that's why! She's half blind. She can't even tell the difference between a famous show dog and a mangy alley mutt!"

The reporters turned their full attention on the awful children, and just like that, no one was paying attention to Masterpiece or Joanie at all. They were alone, surrounded by people, the eye of the storm.

He snuggled into her, so happy he thought he might start barking again. They had made it past the worst danger. Everything would be okay.

But then Joanie stiffened, and the sounds of the crowd changed, and Masterpiece looked up just as Joanie let out a gasp.

Mr. and Mrs. Dayton were standing in the open doorway of Dayton Family Shoeshine, gaping out at the crowd of locals, the wall of media, the count and mayor and upstanding citizens pressed against the front windows of their shop, pure bewilderment written across both their faces.

Twenty-Eight
A MASTERPIECE

Cameras flashed.

The group on the sidewalk drew aside.

The Daytons stood alone.

Mrs. Dayton's wild eyes finally found her daughter. "Joanie!" she said, rushing over. "What's going on? We saw Main Street was blocked, so we came around the back. Only the door—it's broken, and the place is a mess. Were we robbed?" She blinked. "And why are you wearing your good dress?"

"Who are all these people?" asked Mr. Dayton, patting Joanie's arm where it wrapped around Masterpiece. "I'm glad this boy found you, at least. It was the strangest thing: Your mother and I were getting our shoes on when he came barking at the door. When I opened it, he raced into your room and came back with paper or something in his mouth, then ran off this way. Your mother and I thought you might be in trouble!"

It was the most Joanie could remember her father saying all at once in a long time. His face was flushed, like her mother's, and his eyes were very bright.

She was opening her mouth to reply, to try and explain everything that was happening and how she'd gotten herself in the middle of it, when the dog in her arms gave a soft woof and bent forward, licking her chin.

"What is it, Lucky?" she asked. "What do you want to tell me?"

Lucky squirmed until she bent to set him down, and as she did, she spotted the stack of cardboard he had placed at her feet.

She knew what it was as soon as her fingers brushed the top one.

"Why?" she whispered. "What did you bring these for?"

Lucky was prancing back and forth, his tail going wild.

Joanie picked up the pile and stood, three cardboard squares in her hands.

"What have you got there, sweetie?" asked her father. "Is that whatever your dog grabbed from the house?"

Her heart thumping, Joanie turned over the first piece of cardboard.

It was one of her paintings. This one showed a fashion

model Joanie had seen in a magazine, with silver skin and a flowing midnight dress. It was one of Joanie's best.

"Goodness!" said Mrs. Dayton. She reached out a hand, her fingers hovering above the graceful swirls of shoe polish. "But, Joanie, the dog got this out of your bedroom. Where did *you* get it?"

Mr. Dayton was watching his daughter's face. "She made it," he said quietly. "Is that right, Joanie?"

Joanie swallowed hard and nodded. Her big secret was out.

Her mother took the painting, holding it up for a long moment. Joanie held her breath, waiting for a lecture about wasting shoe polish, or time, or dreams.

"It's beautiful," Mrs. Dayton said.

For one shimmering moment, Joanie thought she was about to get her longed-for smile, but a high, trumpeting voice called, "Say, what's that?" and next moment a hand tipped with red nails yanked the painting away from Mrs. Dayton.

The chaos around them came rushing back in.

Holly Knickerbocker gripped the square of cardboard tight, her eyebrows climbing toward her tight brown curls as she examined it. She whistled.

"This is really something," she said, ignoring Mrs. Dayton's request to hand it back. "Hey! Hey, you!" She snapped her fingers at the reporters. "Get a load of this!"

Joanie began to feel dizzy again. She'd only just shown her own parents her top-secret paintings. Things were happening too fast.

"What is that?" demanded Count Pulaski, pushing between Holly and the cameras. "Let me see!" He seized the artwork and gasped. Somewhere around Joanie's feet, Lucky gave an excited yip.

"But this is tremendous!" declared the count. "The styling, the delicate use of light, the beauty!"

He caught sight of Joanie and pulled the rest of the cardboard out of her hands. Holly Knickerbocker, the Archers, and the Payton-Prices all crowded around, peering at it.

"Oh!" gasped Count Pulaski as he turned over the second piece. He held it up. "It's the little dog."

It was Joanie's portrait of Lucky. She hadn't seen it since she'd painted it—was that only two nights ago?—and looking at it now she felt a rush of pride. She really had captured his sweet, wide-eyed expression perfectly.

The locals oohed and aahed while the reporters scratched their heads and asked what was going on. Was this still part of the dognapping story?

Count Pulaski waved for attention.

"I think we have our answer to how this girl made her innocent mistake," he announced. He turned to Joanie, and this time he was smiling. "It was you who created this work of art? Yes?"

Joanie, still tumbling with the turn of events, nodded.

"Well, then all is clear," said the count. "You encountered this stray animal, you fell in love as little girls do, and you painted this portrait because you are an artist. And this"—he brandished the painting—"this is how you see your new pet: He is handsome, he is regal, he is well mannered. And the fact that the rest of us see an awkward, poorly groomed, ill-mannered menace, that does not matter to you. You love him.

"And then yesterday, perhaps, you see the photos of my missing companion in the paper, and you remember this." He tapped the portrait. "Not so unlike, is it? It looks almost something like my beloved friend, who is very famous. And in the eyes of a dreamy little girl, that connection becomes truth!"

He gave Joanie a glowing, full-toothed smile as the crowd and media took in the revelation: It had all been a misunderstanding. Joanie Dayton had not been trying to pull off a hoax. Happy sighs and chuckles ran through the crowd.

Joanie, meanwhile, was seething. That man had called her a "little girl"! Twice! Once more and she was absolutely going to scream.

She pushed forward, ready to snatch her paintings back

and give the man a piece of her mind. How dare he make up stories about her! But something tangled around her feet. She swayed and looked down to see Lucky weaving between her ankles. He gave her the biggest puppy dog eyes ever, opening his mouth in a silent woof.

Clearly, he wanted her to stay where she was. But why?

Beside them, Count Pulaski passed the dog portrait to a reporter and flipped over the final square.

He did not gasp. He did not cheer. He stared at the painting, silent, and so did Holly Knickerbocker, the Archers, the Payton-Prices, and their kids.

The whole group of them stared and stared and stared, until the impatient crowd began calling out to see.

His hand trembling, Count Pulaski held the square of cardboard up, and at last Joanie, her parents, the crowd of locals, and the finest reporters in New York City saw.

It was the portrait of Joanie's mother.

The crowd oohed again, and a babble of excited chatter broke out.

Behind Joanie, someone gasped, then let out a sob.

She turned just as her mother's arms wrapped around her. Joanie hugged her back, and mother and daughter held each other while Lucky leaned happily against her ankles, his tail wagging.

At last they broke apart, and it was Mr. Dayton's turn to

hug Joanie while Mrs. Dayton stared and stared at the picture in Count Pulaski's hands.

"It looks like me," she said, her voice weak.

"It *is* you," Joanie corrected, her father nodding agreement beside her. "It's how you look when—" She broke off, gathering her courage, then spoke what had been weighing on her heart. "It's how you look when you're not sad. When you remember I'm there and smile at me. When you're happy."

For the rest of her life, Joanie would never forget the look her words brought to her mother's face. It was like watching a wave reach the shore, moving from joy to sorrow to regret to love, finally settling on hope, like sunlight on the water after a storm.

Sylvia Dayton looked Joanie full in both eyes—the sharp eye and the soft—and smiled.

Joanie thought her heart might truly burst.

She wanted to prance and run and wag her tail like Lucky. She might not have managed to save their family finances with the reward money, but keeping her friend by her side and getting this smile from her mother? Those were the finest rewards in the world.

Over in the center of the action, Count Pulaski had become locked in a heated discussion with Holly Knickerbocker. Holly had taken charge of Joanie's first two paintings and was waving them in the count's face, while he brandished the portrait of Sylvia Dayton in hers.

Finally, Holly seemed to back down, and Count Pulaski held up a hand, calling the fracturing crowd to attention and silence one last time.

"Friends! Admirers!" he announced grandly. "This has been a remarkable day. We may not have found my beloved missing dog, whose search must and will continue. But we have instead discovered something almost as special." He held the portrait of Joanie's mother high. "As you know, I am a connoisseur of fine art, and have sat on the boards of several museums. It appears the impressionist era has returned to America! We have found a sensational new talent here today, ladies and gentlemen, and while all of Miss Dayton's paintings are remarkable, this painting, in my humble opinion—and if you will pardon the serendipity of the term—is nothing less than a genuine, certified . . . masterpiece!"

There was a pause as the watching crowd drew in their breath.

Then the cameras flashed, and the cheering began.

Epilogue
A GIRL LIKE JOANIE

There was still a week to go before the Fourth of July, but red, white, and blue bunting ran up and down the sunny length of Main Street. The people of Banbridge liked their summer holidays, and for the first time anybody could remember, the banners reached all the way to the small, forgotten shopfront tucked away at the end, the former site of Dayton Family Shoeshine.

The square brick building was still there. The alley beside it still held a jumbled collection of pallets, crates, and paint cans. Tins of shoe polish were still displayed along the windowsills.

Everything else had changed.

Lucky—that was his name now, through and through— sat on his spot in the shoeshine chair in the middle of the front window. The leather was soft and warm, and actually much more comfortable than his old satin pillow in the window of Poodles, Inc. The summer sun shone down, sending the new words painted across the window arcing onto the polished wood floor: THE JOANNE LOUISE DAYTON STUDIO & ART GALLERY.

Lucky sighed contentedly, gazing around at the shop.

The other shoeshine chair had been removed, and the back corner converted into the spot where Joanie's cardboard masterpieces, beautifully lit, were displayed. Mr. Paul Dayton framed each one himself, a talent that let him continue to spend every day at his old shoe repair bench, his beloved tools lined up just so.

Mrs. Sylvia Dayton, her hair in a twist, a simple but chic new dress adding to her movie-star beauty, was greeting and helping the few lucky customers the shop could hold at one time. The rest were lined up outside, just like every weekend since the gallery had opened. Mrs. Dayton smiled often these days, and laughed, too, telling everyone about her talented, remarkable daughter. Her daughter who could look at things from different perspectives any old time she liked.

The wall behind the counter, once plastered with advertisements for waterproofing waxes, was now completely hidden behind framed clippings about Joanie. There were newspapers and magazines from all over the country, and in pride of place, a copy of *LIFE* magazine, the cover showing Joanie in front of the old shoeshine, looking nervous, excited, and pretty as could be in her favorite old best dress. *A Girl Like Joanie: The Remarkable Discovery of an American Genius,* read the headline. *Interviewed by the nation's favorite raconteur: Holly Knickerbocker.*

Holly had been around quite a bit since the incidents in the spring. She had told the world Joanie was her discovery, since she arrived in town first, and had latched onto the family, advising them at length about what a great hook they had with the shoeshine, and how the art world of New York loved a humble origin story. That was why Joanie still used nothing but shoe polish and cardboard, though with the prices her paintings were fetching, she could have had the finest paints and brushes money could buy. But Holly insisted branding was essential, and Joanie loved her familiar shoe polish tins anyway and didn't mind a bit.

As for Count Pulaski, he had bought most of the collection under Joanie's bed, then busily spread the story of *his* discovery of Joanie Dayton as part of the continuing search for his beloved dog. Most of the public had taken his side, but many in the press sided with their colleague Holly Knickerbocker, and the resulting feud had kept the Daytons in the public eye for far longer than anyone would have imagined.

Lucky stretched, shifting slightly so he could move his paws into a patch of sunlight. It was simply marvelous how everything had turned out. He had wanted Joanie to be happy from the first moment he met her, and now, at last, she was.

The happy chatter of customers merged with the sound of the cash register as Mrs. Dayton rang up another sale. Someone gave an exclamation, and Lucky looked up to see Joanie moving aside the curtain that separated the shop from her studio in the back room. People waiting outside craned their necks and pressed their faces to the windows as they spotted her, trying to catch a glimpse of the brand-new work of art in her hands.

Lucky grinned as he noticed the Archers halfway down the line. The mayor had already purchased two of Joanie's pieces for his office in city hall. It looked like he was ready for more. And as for Jerry and Michael there in line with him, well, they had been awfully polite since that day the press came to town, and even begged Joanie to join them for kickball after the whole elementary school watched her being interviewed on the TV.

Joanie had told them she would think about it. She was still deciding.

Lucky lifted his head and sniffed the air. The shop smelled of shoe polish and leather, like before, but now those were joined by the spice of freshly cut wood from Mr. Dayton's workbench, and the sweet touch of Mrs. Dayton's new perfume.

And then there was Joanie. Maybe it was his imagination, but ever since the world had seen her the way he saw her, had seen that this lonely, forgotten, overlooked girl was kind, and honest, and thoughtful, and so wonderfully, bravely herself, Joanie's beautiful sunshine smell had begun to remind him just the tiniest bit of flowers.

She was still the same old Joanie, though. She still wore her overalls or workday dress to paint. She still liked to run around, and explore the alley, and wander the neighborhoods saying hello to her favorite plants. Only now she and Lucky did all those things together. Now the neighbors came out and waved, and the kids they met had questions and compliments instead of put-downs and jokes.

Lucky tilted his head to scratch an ear. He was just about used to his new haircut now. Plenty of time had passed, but Joanie still kept his coat cut as short as possible, occasionally renewing his spots just in case. Maybe eventually people would forget about Masterpiece and he could grow his hair out again. Maybe Count Pulaski would find a new dog to be his star companion. He hoped so. He wished Count Pulaski well.

And it all made sense, in a satisfying kind of way, that he

would have this new look to go along with his new name and new home. He had lived at the height of glamour and fame before, a celebrity among celebrities, and yet he'd never been so contented in his life as he was here, now, sitting on a worn shoeshine chair in a humble shopfront in small-town New Jersey, his family around him, supporting his girl while she followed her dreams.

He knew from his ears to the tip of his tail that he really was lucky. The luckiest dog in the world.

And as for all the days to come, his life ahead with Joanie? Well, he might be just a small-town poodle, but he knew one thing for sure: their future would be a masterpiece.

HISTORICAL NOTE

Great news! Many parts of the story you just read are true.

Masterpiece was a real dog, and poodle entrepreneur Alexi Pulaski (who might not have been an actual count) was his real owner. Masterpiece was born August 4, 1946, and quickly became Pulaski's all-time favorite. Charming, intelligent, and adorable at just eight pounds and nine and a half inches tall, he rose to be a champion on the dog show circuit. But his fame didn't end there. He went on to conquer New York high society and appear in magazines, newspapers, advertisements, and television shows. When a real-life prince offered a fortune to try to buy him for his wife, Masterpiece became known as "the world's most valuable dog."

He really did lead a parade of poodles up Fifth Avenue in Manhattan, and he really did dine with politicians in the finest hotels in Paris. He also had his own bank account, hosted fashion shows, and served as goodwill ambassador to Cuba. America went wild for poodles in the 1950s, and it was due in no small part to Count Pulaski and his mission to make everyone love little Masterpiece as much as he did.

Then, one sunny day in May 1953, Masterpiece vanished

from his usual spot at Poodles, Inc. A monthslong police hunt spread through thirteen states, but no trace of the dog was ever found. Only one witness came forward, claiming to have seen Masterpiece trotting out of Poodles, Inc., of his own free will alongside a dark-haired woman wearing a red coat. That woman, like Masterpiece's whereabouts, remains a mystery to this day.

So, what do you think happened? Was Masterpiece dognapped? Did he leave with a friend? Was he ready to give up his high-fashion life for something simpler? Or did someone make the choice for him?

I wrote this book to give the story of Masterpiece a happy next chapter. A chapter where he goes on an adventure and finds a home, a friend, and all the things he never knew he was missing. Where he finds a girl like Joanie Dayton, and she finds a dog like him. And not a day goes by without scritches.

AUTHOR'S NOTE

Getting to use your imagination might be the best part of being a writer, but one thing I didn't need any imagination for in this book was Joanie's experience with her *soft* and *sharp* eyes. This is a real condition called refractive amblyopia, and I've had it since I was born.

It happens when an eye never learns to focus, so the brain moves all its looking to the one that does. Sometimes this means one eye moves a little separately from the other, a condition commonly known as "lazy eye." Often, the inactive eye's vision registers as legally blind.

I never knew my vision was different from anyone else's until elementary school, when I failed my first eye exam in front of the class. Later, I couldn't get 3D glasses to work. A few kids were mean about it for a while, but in the end I decided I liked my unusual eyes. Just like Joanie, my *sharp* eye is super sharp, and my *soft* eye makes the whole world rich and glowy, like looking through a foggy stained-glass window. Each of my eyes can see something the other can't, and in the end, I think that's pretty cool.

I was a big reader growing up, but I never found books about kids with eyes like mine, which is why I decided to let

Joanie try them out in this one. Believe it or not, she taught *me* a few things, and I had an amazing time seeing Banbridge and Masterpiece and all of it through her. But the most important thing I learned from Joanie is this: Wherever we are, whatever tools we have to work with, it's always worthwhile to slow down and look at things from a different perspective.

Or better still, two.

ACKNOWLEDGMENTS

TK

ABOUT THE AUTHOR

TK